Shifter High

ANTLER TROUBLE

A Shifter High Anthology

Written By
A.J. CULEY

Illustrated By
JEANINE HENNING

Edited by J.L. Troughton

A POOF! Press Publication

for my dad, Michael Joe,
who taught me that laughter is a gift
to be shared with the world

CONTENTS

THE TROUBLE WITH SHIFTER TOWNS (a.k.a. They're Not Human-Proofed)

Shifter High: Season 1, Episode 0

Written By

A.J. CULEY

contents

<u>**one**</u>

desperate times

TOWN HALL

David Peacock peeked into the meeting hall and blanched. It looked as if every single citizen of Shifterville had come to the town meeting. Every single one, from youngest to oldest.

They were going to eat the Town Council alive. And since he was head of that council, and mayor of the town, he didn't expect to survive the first five minutes.

David briefly contemplated fleeing, but where would he go? If he showed up in any shifter town worldwide, he'd be scorned as the shifter mayor who fled his own constituents. And pretending to be a human, living among the sad and wretched who had no animals within, was out of the question. He shuddered. He'd rather die.

He groaned at the thought, for he was pretty sure it was going to come to that, then turned to the rest of the Council. "I guess we should get out there."

Maggie Fox rolled her eyes. "You think?" She shoved past

David and led the way into the packed town hall.

Five minutes later, the five council members were seated at the table elevated at the front of the room.

David grabbed the glass of water at his seat and gulped it down. He wondered what he'd been thinking when he ran for mayor. If he'd just stayed a council member, he wouldn't be in the hot seat right now, the one at the center of the table with two members on either side of him. He would have been able to just sit back and let someone else explain the situation they were in to the crowds of nearly feral shifters.

He wondered briefly if Joe Grizzly, who sat at the end to his right would manage to save him from being torn apart when the predators attacked.

For that matter, David was pretty sure some of the prey animals in the room would be even more vicious than their predator counterparts. Those gophers had sharp teeth.

And the *rabbits*.

David shuddered.

Maggie leaned across Steve Armadillo who sat on his left and growled, "David, if you don't get this show on the road, my fox is going to bite your feathers off!"

David gulped. He could feel his eyes widening with panic and he grabbed the microphone in front of him, cleared his throat and started babbling. He had no idea what he said, but everyone in the room eventually settled into their seats and fell silent.

"So. Um." David shook his head, trying desperately to get his thoughts in order, then stumbled through a brief explanation of why they had called this meeting. "The Town Council has already met numerous times about this issue. Um. The vet issue I mean. We even made a decision, but then–" He glanced at the rest of the Town Council members. "–we realized we couldn't be responsible for this decision alone. We need your input. All of you. This is the kind of thing where we all have to agree and be on board or–" He stopped, uncertain how to continue.

"Or what?" Liza Crane demanded.

"Or we don't hire a vet."

"What?" A cacophony of sound exploded as everyone leapt to their feet and started shouting.

"We need a vet!"

"I feel another furball coming on right now!" Laney Siamese wailed. She raised a hand to her throat and hunched her shoulders.

"Stop these ridiculous excuses!" Melissa Siamese shouted as she wrapped an arm around her daughter's shoulders. "Just hire a hacking vet already!"

"Yeah!" There was a chorus of agreements.

Great. The masses were agreeing with the Siamese.

This was terrible.

The end of the world as they knew it.

"We didn't have this issue when Hardy was hired," one of the many rabbit residents shouted.

"There's something seriously wrong with this council if they can't even make a simple decision like this," another rabbit agreed.

"Just hire someone! *Anyone!*" A huge lion shifter roared from the back, making David's shoulders hunch.

Lions.

They gave him heartburn.

"Yeah!" The shouts in the audience got louder until David could literally feel his blood pressure spiking.

Just hire someone? He grabbed the milk carton at his feet and slammed it on the table. "Just hire someone?"

The room fell silent as the tower of paper stacked inside the milk carton wobbled and tilted to the side. The paper seemed to hang there for a moment, then the top of the stack slid right off and scattered across the table, papers flying everywhere.

"This carton is full of all the email requests we've received since Hardy left us six months ago." David reached into the carton and pulled out the rest of the stack that had been on top. "These are requests for a predator vet." He slammed the stack onto the table, then grabbed the next stack and slammed it down beside the first one. Though smaller than the original stack, it was still an impressive tower of papers. "These are prey vet requests." He then tilted the milk carton toward the audience so everyone could see it was still half full. "And *these* are all the requests for a vet who specializes in specific ailments like ingrown claws and premature fur loss and–and–" He caught sight of Laney and her mother glaring at him from the front of the crowd. "–and furballs!"

A few chuckles and titters of nervous laughter came from the audience.

Melissa Siamese whirled and glared at the offenders, who fell instantly silent under the force of her glare.

David swallowed nervously, then continued. "So you tell us. How are we supposed to *just hire someone* and have them meet all these ridiculous, conflicting requests?"

Silence.

"That's what I thought," David muttered. He glared at the crowd and admitted, "Meeting these demands is impossible, for more than one reason, but mostly because after six months of searching, we still only have one applicant."

And everyone was off again.

"Only one?"

"But that's crazy!"

"Surely there are more vets looking for work than just one!"

"Well, who is this one applicant?" Melissa Siamese demanded.

"Yeah!" A chorus of agreements followed.

"Is he prey?" Bob Gazelle asked.

"Is she a predator?" Tiffany Hyena called out.

Mayor Peacock held up a hand to quiet the crowd. "This particular applicant has a huge list of specializations and quite a few degrees. He's worked on small and large animals of all kinds." He hesitated, then continued, "he's worked for farms, zoos, wildlife preserves, small clinics, big clinics. To be honest, he's had more experience than Hardy did when the previous Council hired him."

"Well, what's the holdup?" Debbie Panda threw her arms in the air. "He sounds perfect!"

David rolled his eyes. Debbie was just sick of working with Murdock Mallard whose lack of quacking sense when it came to animal ailments made her crazy. Of course, Debbie would leap at the chance to work with a real vet again, no matter who it was.

"Hold on just a minute," Sally Wolf said. "A shifter vet working on a farm?"

"Forget the farm! What about the zoo?" Max Lemur asked.

"Yeah! Did he set all the animals free?" Karly Bat wondered.

"Oh, who cares about all that?" Murdock Mallard asked impatiently. "He's qualified. I say hire him!"

"I agree!" Debbie shouted.

"Now hold on a minute. What exactly *are* his specializations? Has he studied furballs, that's what I want to know!" Laney Siamese exclaimed.

"That's not the most important question," Bethany Pterodactyl snapped at Laney. She whirled on the council. "He *is* a predator, right?"

"I hope not!" James Mole said. "A predator vet would never understand our needs as prey."

"That's why Hardy was so perfect," Lisa Mole said. "He was a prey animal who understood our natures and was super gentle with us."

"Yeah," Jake Tiger said. "He wasn't scared of us predators either."

"And he didn't act like prey!" Katrina Tiger agreed with her brother.

"All right, all right!" Mayor Peacock raised his voice to be heard over the chorus of agreements. "Look. I've emailed Hardy. Numerous times. Begging him to come back. Do you hear me? I begged. But he said no. We're not getting him back and there just aren't any other giraffe vets looking for work." Or *any* shifter vets for that matter.

"Well who's this applicant then?" Debbie demanded.

"He's a predator, right?" Bethany asked.

"No, he's not a predator."

All the prey animals cheered.

"He's hired!" Harold Mouse shouted.

Mayor Peacock rolled his eyes. "Calm down. It's not that easy. He's not prey either."

"What?"

"How can that be?"

"That doesn't even make sense!"

"Well, I'm a predator," Mandy Seal said. "But I'm also the prey of other animals like polar bears, so—"

Everyone looked at Mayor Peacock, but he shook his head. "It's not that. Well, it might be." He thought about that a minute.

Did anyone hunt humans?

Surely not.

"They're carnivorous," he said decisively. Then a moment later, "Or maybe they're omnivores. I don't think they're herbivores."

"Ugh. That means they're predators," Doris Rabbit whispered.

"I don't think so," Mayor Peacock said. "I mean. Well." He

glanced at the council members helplessly. How could he possibly explain this?

"Oh for heaven's sake, David." Maggie leaned forward and grabbed one of the microphones. "Stop beating around the bush and just tell them." She stared straight at Melissa Siamese and said directly into the microphone, "The only applicant for the job is a human."

To: Mayor Peacock

From: Dr. Murdock Mallard

Subject: Please help!

Mayor Peacock, I'm begging you.

I simply cannot continue this farce any longer. Day after day attempting to treat ailments like mange and hacking furball syndrome – it's a complete disgrace! A waste of my degrees and credentials. Even worse, I'm failing my patients in every way, whether they come to me in human form or shifted ones.

Let's be clear. I'm a medical doctor who specializes in human ailments, not animal ones, and as such am singularly unqualified to provide hoof and claw trims. I am also, quite frankly, not a miracle worker!

Please hire a veterinarian immediately, before I go quacking mad.

Sincerely Yours,

Shifterville's one and only medical doctor, who is now contemplating the human organization, Doctors Without Borders, as a viable career alternative

To: Shifterville Town Council

From: Melissa Siamese

Subject: This situation has gotten out of hand!

It's time to make a decision! Are you our town council or are you a bunch of wishy-washy humans?

My daughter, Laney, has been hacking up furballs every night for two weeks. And do you think that quack of a doctor, Mallard what's-his-name, knows anything about furballs? Of course, he doesn't!

He's not treating the ailment at all. Instead, he had the gall to suggest Laney stop grooming herself in cat form and instead simply take a shower! A shower! Can you imagine? A siamese cat bathing? In water? Why we'd be the laughingstock of all Siamese shifters everywhere. We have a reputation to uphold, you know!

Figure this out at once or be prepared to lose every election from here to the end of time!

To: Shifterville Town Council

From: bunny1985@preynetwork.com

Subject: Vet Request

Dear Town Council,

I'm certain you will not be surprised to hear that many of your citizens, most especially those of a prey nature, are experiencing some anxiety around the hiring of a new vet.

The truth is Hardy Giraffe was an amazing vet, quite compassionate and caring. In addition, being a prey animal himself, he was extraordinarily patient and understanding of the anxieties many prey animals experience when going in for routine check-ups, let alone when yearly vaccinations are due.

As such, we would like to request another prey veterinarian be hired for this position. If we cannot lure Hardy back from his retirement, we feel another prey shifter vet is the next best thing.

Sincerely, the prey citizens of Shifterville

To: Mayor Peacock
From: laney@siamese.com
Subject: furballs are killing me!

Dear Mayor Peacock,

Are you aware of how incredibly uncomfortable it is to have a furball stuck in your chest? To feel it rising from the depths to catch in your throat? To have to hack that thing up? Worse, to hack up multiples, one after the other?

Before Dr. Giraffe left town, he wrote me an ongoing prescription for my furball medicine. The refills ran out five weeks ago! And I've been hacking up furballs ever since.

When Dr. Giraffe wrote that prescription, he never expected me to have to use all those refills before the town hired a specialist. This is ridiculous! Did you know that Dr. Giraffe told me that it might take time for the Town Council to find the right vet, especially one that specializes in furballs, but he was certain you were up to the task.

A week, he said, maybe two. Three at most. Well, it's been months! And I'm tired of the feel of fur in my throat.

No more excuses.

Hire the promised furball specialist now!

To: Hardy Giraffe
From: Mayor Peacock
Subject: Please come back!

Dear Hardy,

I know you're finally enjoying retirement in the wilds of Africa, but I'm certain you miss us by now. We sure do miss you. The town just isn't the same without you, Hardy.

Look, I'll be honest. We're in a real pickle. One heck of a prickly mess of a pickle.

I've only got one applicant for your job and he's human! What am I supposed to do, Hardy? It's not like I can hire the human!

We're under real pressure here.

Any minute the entire populace is going to revolt and we'll all be out of a job. We still won't have a vet, though, so I don't know how threatening our jobs is going to solve this problem, but there you have it. All our jobs are on the line!

I don't mean to be rude, Hardy, but couldn't you have waited a tiny bit longer? Given us a chance to find your replacement before leaving us in the lurch?

I mean, sure, you did wait three years, but what would another three have hurt? I suppose you figured you were ninety-three and had earned your retirement, but Hardy, we needed you! We still need you.

And honestly, I don't think the people are going to wait around much longer.

Forget the election. I may not survive the next month.

These people are vicious. I'm just a peacock, Hardy!

I don't have a chance against the tigers and the grizzlies and lord those Siamese. They're just mean!

Please, Hardy, I'm begging you.

Come back!

To: Mayor Peacock

From: Hardy Giraffe

Subject: Re: Please come back!

No.

To: Hardy Giraffe

From: Mayor Peacock

Subject: Re: Re: Please come back!

Well do you have any suggestions? Any recommendations? Colleagues looking for work?

To: Mayor Peacock

From: Hardy Giraffe

Subject: Re: Re: Re: Please come back!

All my colleagues are either dead or retired and they've been so for a lot longer than me. So no. I don't have any recommendations.

To: Mayor Peacock

From: Hardy Giraffe

Subject: Re: Re: Re: Please come back!

I take it back. I do have one.

Hire the human.

two

the plan

"WELL THAT WENT swimmingly," Joe Grizzly said glumly.

"What are we going to do?" David asked. He couldn't get the look on his wife's face out of his head. Or his mother's. The minute Maggie had announced the applicant was human, his wife had grinned so big, he was shocked she hadn't started laughing right there. He was pretty sure she was delighted because his mother, who was sitting right next to her, looked like she might burst from her human skin at any moment. His wife would have loved that.

His mother was old school, proper about everything, and so damn judgmental, Maribeth would have been delighted to see her mother-in-law lose her feathers in front of the entire town.

Of course, his mother had maintained rigid control, though she'd glared at him the rest of the meeting. She hadn't said a word, but he knew he'd hear all about this later. How he would be the mayor to ruin Shifterville with his radical ideas. Like he was the one who went and recruited George Finch or something. It wasn't his fault only a human wanted the job!

"David?"

He jumped. The rest of the Town Council was staring at him, waiting for him to say something. "What?"

Maggie rolled her eyes. "We were discussing next steps."

"Oh right. And what did you decide?"

"Not a chance," Steve Armadillo said. "We're not making this decision without you. And you, as our fearless leader, get to announce the decision to the rest of the town."

David shook his head. "No way. Did you see the way they reacted? No way are we going to be the ones responsible for bringing a human to town. We can't. If anything goes wrong, they won't vote us out. They'll maul us to death."

"He's right," Jessica Canary said. "It's why we had the meeting in the first place. Not that it solved anything given all the arguments and the inevitable brawling."

Steve made a disgusted sound. "Bears." He blanched. "Uh, sorry, Joe."

Joe just shook his head. "Whatever."

"We need to give them time," Maggie said. "They'll discuss things and either decide they can wait for us to find the right vet or they can't."

Steve groaned. "So the emails are going to continue?"

"I can't even get through my inbox anymore," Jessica complained. "All those ranting emails are clogging up everything. Even my Tweeter feed is full of birds chirping at me about our lack of a vet."

"We didn't even get around to discussing the pros and cons of hiring the human," David lamented.

"That's okay," Maggie said, "because I have a plan to convince the town that hiring the human is *their* idea."

"Wait. What?" Steve looked horrified.

"That's great," Jessica said. "This has already dragged on way too long."

"I agree," Steve said. "The entire application process is for the birds–" he stumbled to a stop at the look on Jessica's face.

David shook his head. For someone who had to talk to teens and their parents all the time, Steve still managed to put his hoof in his mouth on a regular basis.

Steve winced. "Sorry, Jessica."

She rolled her eyes and waved a hand for him to continue.

He cleared his throat. "Anyway, I'm all in favor of getting someone hired as quickly as possible so we can all move on with our lives, but are we seriously considering hiring a *human*?"

"If the town thinks it's a good idea," Maggie said, "why not?"

No one had a good answer, though David could see everyone was thinking exactly what he was.

This was going to be a nightmare.

To: Jennifer Siamese
From: Melissa Siamese
Subject: You'll never believe it!

I know you're always saying my town is the craziest town you've ever heard of, but they've gone and done it this time, Jennifer. It's beyond crazy. It's downright insane!

Wait. That means crazy too. Well, you know what I mean. Whatever word means crazy times a million, that's where we're at now. I was thinking it might be time for us to finally move, but Laney loves it here. I hate to uproot her from her friends, especially now that she's in high school. Besides, if I leave, who knows what crazy plan this town will come up with next.

Oh, Jennifer, I don't even know how to tell you this latest news.

Brace yourself.

The town council just suggested we hire a human for our open vet position. Can you imagine? A human treating shifter ailments? It's appalling!

To: Melissa Siamese

From: Jennifer Siamese

Subject: Re: You'll never believe it!

Wait. What?

That's absurd. I don't even think that's legal.

Is it?

To: Jennifer Siamese

From: Melissa Siamese

Subject: Re: Re: You'll never believe it!

Apparently it's a gray area.

To: Jennifer Siamese

From: Melissa Siamese

Subject: Re: Re: Re: You'll never believe it!

A gray area??

What does that even mean?

How can there be gray areas in law?

To: Jennifer Siamese

From: Melissa Siamese

Subject: Re: Re: Re: Re: You'll never believe it!

I have no idea. It's simply shameful what shifters get away with nowadays!

To: Debbie Panda

From: Stella Flamingo

Subject: Is it true?

Did you attend the Town Council meeting last night? I can't believe what people are saying. Did the Council really suggest we hire a human for our vet position?

Because that's just crazy! We can't invite humans to town! How would we keep them from discovering the truth? Blind them so they don't notice when we shift into our animals? This is a crazy plan!

Tell me it isn't true!

To: Stella Flamingo
From: Debbie Panda
Subject: Re: Is it true?

Look, Stella, I know shifters are upset, but here's the thing:

Six MONTHS we've been without a vet. That's me, in the vet's office, all by myself, calling the medical doctor every time someone walks in with a complaint.

Dr. Mallard may be a nice guy and he's a great doctor, but he's not qualified to heal our animal sides. Plus it takes him forever to get from one side of town to the other. You'd think he'd choose to move his practice here for a while, or let me move there, but oh no! He doesn't want to give the impression that he's willing to do this long term. So instead he inconveniences me and everyone else.

But do you think anyone complains to him? Of course not! They don't want to upset our only remaining medical professional in town. So instead they whine to me.

We need a vet, Stella. Someone qualified. And I don't care if they're a shifter, a human or an alien, as long as they know how to treat Laney Siamese's hacking furball syndrome and Shane Wolf's flea infestation!

So if this human's our only option, I'll take him! No regrets.

To: Debbie Panda

From: Stella Flamingo

Subject: Re: Re: Is it true?

You're crazy. But I get it. Here's hoping a shifter applies soon, before we're all stuck with the human.

To: Karl Grizzly

From: Alexa Saber

Subject: A human?

What is your brother thinking? Don't you share war stories from the high school with him? What am I saying? Of course you do, which means he knows exactly how dangerous this plan is!

For shift's sake, I heard the vet has a teenaged daughter! Tell me it isn't true, Karl.

Why on earth didn't Joe stop this?

To: Alexa Saber

From: Karl Grizzly

Subject: Re: A human?

You know, just because we're grizzlies doesn't mean we have superpowers.

You do realize that our esteemed principal is also on the Town Council, right? If he couldn't stop them from making this suggestion, I highly doubt my brother could.

Besides, it's not a done deal. From what I understand, the Council was just explaining things. They're not really going to hire the human. *Especially* if he has a teenaged daughter.

I told Joe there was no way we could guarantee the girl's safety and it would only be a matter of time before she was hunted and probably eaten.

Trust me, Ms. Saber, there's no way our Town Council would risk that. The potential political fallout alone will keep them in line.

To: Joe Grizzly
From: Karl Grizzly
Subject: This is your fault.

Thanks a lot, brother.

Alexa Saber has been emailing me all week about this situation. Have you ever had to spend time with a saber-toothed tiger? Especially one who's an English teacher? That woman's scary!

I've spent hours constructing my responses, trying to make sure everything's perfect. Correct spelling, punctuation, no fragments or missing words – it's a pain in the rump!

As if that weren't challenging enough, now she wants to meet in person to discuss things! What is there left to discuss I ask. I've already assured her there's no way the Town Council would ever approve the hiring of a human, but she insists we need to prepare for the worst.

So I'm begging you, Joe. Please don't make a liar out of me. I really don't want to get mauled by her tiger. Or have her rip me to shreds with her words. Either is possible. *Both* are entirely probable.

In fact, if you could get the Town Council to make a public announcement that the human will *not* be hired, that would go a long way toward getting me out of this meeting.

You have to save me, Joe!

To: Karl Grizzly

From: Joe Grizzly

Subject: Re: This is your fault.

Hahahahahahahahahahahahahahahahahahaha.

You're on your own, brother.

To: Joe Grizzly

From: Karl Grizzly

Subject: Re: Re: This is your fault.

You suck.

To: Shifterville Town Council

From: Ms. Helena Squirrel

Subject: Your Proposal

I must say your proposal to hire a human vet is an intriguing one.

Why, just imagine the possibilities! From a purely academic standpoint, the research potential is endless!

The chance to study humans up close, as they adapt to living (unknowingly) in a shifter town, would be a once-in-a-lifetime opportunity. Why just the research question of how humans manage to survive, sanity intact, without an animal inside them could take decades to answer.

Still, I cannot ignore the reality of what this would mean for shifters everywhere. Bringing humans to town would be a disaster. There's no way we could keep the truth from them long-term!

Quite frankly, and I'm sorry to use this language, but your suggestion is absolutely asinine! You'll just have to keep searching because a human is out of the question!

To: Ms. Helena Squirrel
From: Shifterville Town Council
Subject: Re: Your Proposal

Ms. Squirrel,

Please be reassured that we have no intention of inviting humans to our community. We simply mentioned the human applicant as a means of explaining why we had not yet hired a vet.

Obviously, that one applicant is unacceptable. We will simply all have to be patent as we continue our search.

Hopefully we will have a new vet before the end of the year.

To: Ms. Helena Squirrel

From: Stephanie Crane

Subject: Re: vet situation

Did they really say the end of the year?

It can't possibly take that long!

Can it?

To: Stephanie Crane
From: Ms. Helena Squirrel
Subject: Re: Re: vet situation

I honestly don't know. We're at six months now and they only have the one applicant.

I'm starting to think a year may be too optimistic.

To: Shifterville Town Council

From: Melissa Siamese

Subject: Are you stupid?

I mean seriously. What is wrong with you people?

We've been waiting months for a vet and now you suggest we hire a human? You should be ashamed of yourselves! Risking the lives of shifters everywhere just to take the easy way out and hire the first applicant to the job.

Well, we won't stand for it!

The residents of this town aren't going to fall for your attempts to circumvent the requirements of your positions. You're tasked with ensuring our town has all the basic requirements for health and safety. A competent, shifter vet is the very least you can provide!

To: Melissa Siamese

From: Shifterville Town Council

Subject: Re: Are you stupid?

We completely agree.

Hiring a human for any position in town, no matter how competent or qualified they are, would be the height of stupidity, which is why we have already rejected this applicant.

We will continue our search in the hopes that we have a vet hired before the new year. In the meantime, should your daughter's furball condition worsen, we recommend The Rodentville Animal Clinic.

To: Shifterville Town Council

From: Melissa Siamese

Subject: Re: Re: Are you stupid?

Rodentville?

Are you serious?

We Siamese do not visit *rodents* for health care.

To: Melissa Siamese

From: Shifterville Town Council

Subject: Re: Re: Re: Are you stupid?

Oh, of course not. We weren't suggesting that at all. We were simply reminding you that the closest clinic with a qualified shifter vet on staff is in Rodentville.

To: Shifterville Town Council

From: Melissa Siamese

Subject: Re: Re: Re: Re: Are you stupid?

They're one hundred and fifty miles away!

To: Melissa Siamese

From: Shifterville Town Council

Subject: Re: Re: Re: Re: Re: Are you stupid?

True. But still closer than Grizzly Town.

Of course, if you prefer not to travel, you can certainly continue to see Dr. Mallard.

We'll keep you posted on the applicant situation (no change as of yet).

To: Jennifer Siamese

From: Melissa Siamese

Subject: You are not going to believe this!

Now the Town Council is claiming they never mentioned *hiring* the human and we simply have to be patient! Patient! Like we haven't already been patient enough?

It's been six months! If they don't figure things out soon, I'm going to make it my mission in life to get all of them voted out of office, especially that pompous peacock mayor!

I might even jump into the running myself. Just imagine what a Siamese could do for this town!

three

the rumor

THE RUMOR BEGAN in first hour.

Laney Siamese had been sneaking around like cats often do and apparently overheard several teachers discussing the issue of the human vet and his teenaged daughter. And just like that, the news was out.

Karl Grizzly had no idea how so many people knew this man had a teenaged daughter when Karl hadn't even known before Ms. Saber's email.

He blamed his brother.

And the rest of the Council, of course, but mainly just Joe. Because he could.

The news of the human teenager raced around the school, causing an uproar among the students, which of course, made Karl's job all the harder.

P.E. was one of the very few classes where students were allowed to shift on school grounds. It was also *the* only class where both prey and predator students were allowed to shift in each other's presence. The result was sometimes chaotic, but it allowed the students a safe zone to practice control in their shifted forms.

Of course, today was not the day anyone was feeling in control.

The predators were all in hunting mode which just made the prey animals extra jumpy.

If this was how the teens reacted to just the *thought* of a human classmate, Karl shuddered to imagine what the reality would be like. He wanted to believe the Town Council would be smarter than this, that they'd never entertain hiring a human, but despite his assurances to Ms. Saber, he really wasn't that certain.

At that moment, the silence was broken with a tiger's roar and there was a rush of movement as several rabbits, a hedgehog and even a wolf hurtled by, a tiger lunging in their wake.

"Katrina Tiger!" Karl stormed after the tiger and her scattering prey.

Katrina skid to a stop, flung a look over her shoulder at him, then turned and snapped her teeth one last time at the bunnies and hedgehog all cringing behind the growling wolf.

She faced him again, then lunged and stretched upward, morphing back into her human form.

Karl quickly lifted his eyes above her head. Shifters weren't really all that concerned about nudity since everyone came out of the shift naked. Still, this was awkward.

"Locker room, Katrina," he growled.

She huffed and stormed past, shouting as she went, "If that

human enrolls at Shifter High, I won't be held responsible for my tiger's actions. She's a hunter. We hunt!"

Oh yeah. This was a fabulous idea. He was going to kill Joe.

Melvin Moose was slouched down in his chair at the very back of Stephanie Crane's classroom, looking for all the world like he was trying to disappear. An impossible feat at the moment.

Stephanie wanted to yell at him to get his rack under control, but he looked absolutely miserable. Not to mention, Laney Siamese had just entered the room, so really, he was about to be punished enough.

"Oh, that's just great," Laney said loudly. "Here the Town Council's talking about bringing humans to town and there's Melvin Moose unable to control even a partial shift. We're all doomed, people. If those humans come to town, mark my words. Our secret's done for and it will all be Melvin's fault."

Melvin scowled but didn't say anything.

Stephanie figured he didn't know how to defend himself since Laney wasn't saying anything that wasn't true.

If the humans did come to town, it was pretty much a done deal that Melvin would be the one to out shifters worldwide. This was a terrible idea.

"If the human doesn't freak out at the sight of his antlers," Laney sneered, "she'll probably have a breakdown surrounded by so many predators. Pathetic."

"That's enough, Laney," Stephanie said. "Have a seat."

Laney's right, Melvin messaged his best friend Paulie Porcupine. *I'll be reviled worldwide as the moose who revealed our existence to humans.*

Don't be ridiculous, Paulie messaged back. *All you'll have to do is avoid being around her. Besides, it's not like it's going to happen for real or anything. The Town Council will never-never allow it.*

Haven't you been listening to our friends at all? I mean, some of us are upset, sure, but most of the kids think it's the best idea ever. They're excited to meet a human. There's an entire plan in place for kids to talk to their parents about the benefits of hiring the human.

What? That's ridiculous! Why would anyone want a human for a vet-vet?

I don't know. Because it's the most exciting thing that's ever happened in Shifterville?

Well. Probably. Still. It's a terrible-terrible idea.

Of course it is, but people are desperate for a vet. Melvin glared at the bane of his existence, then added, *I think even Laney's in on the plan. All she can talk about lately is the need for a "furball specialist."*

Ha! She's in for a surprise then because I don't think humans get furball-furballs.

To: Jennifer Siamese
From: Melissa Siamese
Subject: Still no vet…

Laney came home from school today talking about the benefits of hiring the human vet. She kept going on and on about his expertise in animal ailments. Apparently this man is some kind of genius. He's studied and worked with all sorts of animals and has more degrees than a dog has fleas. Laney's quite convinced he can help ease her furball suffering.

As for me, I'm really not sold on the idea of a human vet. However, having said that, it does rather strain my patience that the Town Council has refused to act on the one qualified vet application they have, simply because the man is human. Why it's the height of bigotry, and you know we Siamese don't tolerate bigotry in any form!

To: Shifterville Town Council

From: Melissa Siamese

Subject: How long is this going to take?

What exactly are you waiting for? An engraved invitation?

If the human is the only qualified applicant, he's clearly the right choice. So hire him already!

To: All Shifterville Residents

From: Shifterville Town Council

First, an update on the town veterinary position. Unfortunately, we have received no new applicants, which leaves us with the same dilemma we presented at our last town meeting: hire the human or continue the search.

We initially decided in favor of continuing the search, a decision our town's residents seemed to be in agreement with. However, the reality is there are very few shifter vets willing to cross the prey-predator boundary when serving their clientele. After all, what prey veterinarian wants to risk healing a cranky predator? And what predator vet wants to take the chance of losing control and eating his clients?

Shifterville is unique in that both prey and predators live together in relative peace. We were lucky in finding Hardy Giraffe so many decades ago, for he was uniquely suited to serve both predator and prey species alike. We are uncertain we will ever find a shifter vet willing to do the same again.

In addition, it has come to our attention, through a barrage of emails, that the residents of Shifterville may be leaning toward hiring the human after all. Even so, we feel very strongly that this is a decision the Town Council cannot make alone.

Therefore, we will be holding a vote next week at Town Hall.

Voting will commence Sunday at noon and will continue through the following Saturday, until every adult citizen of Shifterville has cast their vote. In addition, because the human vet has a teenaged daughter who would attend Shifter High if the humans move to town, we are also inviting all Shifter High students to participate.

It is important for every resident of Shifterville to understand that a vote of yes will require significant change for the town and its residents. We will all have to work together to ensure the humans never discover our secret.

Please do not vote frivolously. Instead, cast your vote with a full understanding of the issue at hand. Examine the attached Pros and Cons sheet very carefully before making a decision. Please know that every individual vote is important and will have significant impact on the future of Shifterville and the lives of all its residents.

Thank you.

THE VOTE: SHOULD SHIFTERVILLE HIRE A HUMAN VETERINARIAN?

PROS	CONS
1. After months of searching, we'll finally have a vet.	1. George Finch has a teenaged daughter who would have to attend Shifter High.
2. The applicant has several graduate degrees in zoology, wildlife biology and chemistry, as well as a doctorate in veterinary medicine.	2. It's entirely possible (perhaps even probable) that the humans would be eaten, or at least mauled, by one of the town predators.
3. Though human, the applicant has experience working with prey animals and predators of all kinds.	3. Shifter High and the entire town would have to be human-proofed to keep our secrets safe.
4. There have been no shifter applicants to the vet position, despite it being posted for six months now. If we delay in hiring the human, we may lose the opportunity to do so and there's no guarantee we'll get any more applicants, shifter or otherwise.	4. Every single resident of Shifterville, from youngest to oldest, would have to commit to keeping their shifter status secret from the humans. This would mean, at the bare minimum, never shifting around them. Ever.

This overview has been provided to you by your Town Council.

four

the vote

"THIS WAS A brilliant idea," Maggie said.

"How do you figure?" David asked. The lines outside had grown to mammoth proportions. It looked like every single shifter citizen had shown up for the vote on the very first day.

"If they vote no to the human vet, we're off the hook!" Maggie exclaimed. "They can't complain if it takes us another six months to find the right vet because they voted no to the one applicant we had."

"And if they vote yes?" Jessica asked.

"Then we're not the ones responsible if anything goes wrong. They'll only have themselves to blame."

"Have you *met* the Siamese?" David demanded. "They would blame us for the stars in the sky if it was to their advantage!"

"True," Joe said. "And no matter how the vote turns out, they won't be happy."

"This is going to be a nightmare," Steve said.

To: All Shifterville Residents

From: Shifterville Town Council

First, we would like to thank all Shifterville residents for participating in the recent vote on the hiring of a new vet. Never doubt this was perhaps the most historic vote ever held in a shifter town.

By an overwhelming majority, the town has voted in favor of hiring the human vet.

We, your town council, have mixed feelings about this. We feel your urgency to have a competent vet in town. On the other hand, we fear the changes we will see in our community as a result of this vote.

Despite our misgivings and fears (which we are certain you also share), we will extend the offer to George Finch immediately, and will keep you informed of his response.

Thank you again for your participation in the vote!

To: All Shifterville Residents

From: Shifterville Town Council

We are pleased to announce that the human, George Finch, has accepted our offer.

He and his daughter, Amelia, will move to our town mid-August, just in time for Amelia to begin her first year at Shifter High. This means we have three short months to prepare for this historic event.

We cannot stress enough the importance of guarding our secret from the humans. As we prepare for their arrival, please discuss this event with everyone in your family. It is of particular importance for the little ones to understand they must never reveal their shifter sides to the humans.

Please keep an eye out for future memos detailing what to expect as we prepare for this historic event.

To: All Shifterville Residents

From: Shifterville Town Council

As Shifterville prepares itself for its newest (and first human) residents, we would like to remind you of the challenges our town faces in the coming months.

Because it is absolutely critical the humans remain unaware of our existence, we must work together to ensure our newest residents never discover our secret. This work begins now, as we prepare for their arrival.

Therefore, please adhere to the following rules as we begin our preparations.

1. Shifting in public is now prohibited. If you wish to roam the town in your natural, animal form, you must first shift in private.

2. You must remain in your human form in all public access buildings. This includes all restaurants, stores and, most especially, the schools. The only exception to this rule is Physical Education classes, where it will be permitted for students to continue dressing out in fur as usual.

3. If you are injured in animal form, someone in human form must take you to the vet's office, to maintain the pretense that we are a community of caregivers for a variety of animals. In other words, no shifting to human form to explain an ailment, then shifting back to animal

form for treatment. Our human vet, Dr. Finch, will figure things out very quickly should you try this.

4. From now on, our town shall be referred to as Shifferville – two Fs, no T. All signs on public buildings will be updated to reflect this change. For example, Shifter Library is now to be known as Shiffer Library. Please begin using this terminology immediately.

5. It is now strictly prohibited to indulge in partial shifts in any public space where a human might become witness to such an event. In other words, Melvin Moose, gain control of your rack!

The following is a list of the buildings that will be remodeled this summer, to ensure a more human-friendly town environment. Please have patience with the crews as they carry out this very important work.

Shiffer Books

Shiffer Café and Restaurant

Shiffer Courthouse

Shiffer Elementary School

Shiffer Grocery

Shiffer High School

Shiffer Ice Cream Parlor

Shiffer Library

Shiffer Middle School

Shiffer Pharmacy

Shiffer Sheriff's Department

Shiffer Town Hall

Shiffer Veterinarian Office

Additionally, a new bowling alley and movie theater will be built off the square on Main Street. We have it on good authority these are highly popular, human entertainments. Once construction is complete, we hope families will visit these establishments, so as to give them an authentic, well-used air.

Thank you for your adherence to these rules and your assistance in this difficult process.

the humans are coming

THIS WAS PERHAPS the worst summer job Karl Grizzly had ever accepted. Usually during summer vacation, when school was out of session, he did some coaching and various odd jobs around the town to help out. This time, though, the town needed members for its newly formed Human-Proofing Committee.

Karl had accepted because it paid well and seemed an excellent use of his time since it would give him a better understanding of how well prepared the town was for the arrival of the humans (not very) and how much work there was left to be done (way more than was reasonable). He hoped the information he gathered on the job would keep Alexa Saber from driving him nuts all summer long (he wasn't holding his breath though).

Today's task involved changing the town's signs. The committee began at the grocery store and worked its way around the town square. As they journeyed from business to business, a pattern began to emerge.

The grocery store owner demanded to know who was going to

teach Melvin Moose to control his partial shifts.

The bookstore owner complained about Melvin knocking over a display of new books when one of the Rabbit girls walked by.

People at the pharmacy, the library, the sheriff's department and the town hall all had similar complaints and demands.

At the cafe, Karl's brother Max glared at him and muttered, "Traitor," as the committee set to work changing the cafe's sign.

For once, though, Karl wasn't bothered by his brother's attitude. Instead, Karl was counting his blessings because it looked like he might actually get away without hearing Melvin's name this time.

Then his sister-in-law, Stella, demanded to know whether he'd spoken with the moose lately. "That boy got stuck in the doors the other day, half in and half out, antlers caught on the door jam, and all because a couple teenaged girls were trying to enter the cafe at the same time he was exiting. You're the Human-Proofing Committee, aren't you? So how are you going to human-proof his antlers?"

Of course, as usual, Karl had no answers, so instead, he just promised, like he'd done with every other person who had approached him that day, that he would speak with Melvin and impress upon him the importance of learning to control his rack.

Still, Karl knew no matter how many people spoke to Melvin about his control issues, it wouldn't change a thing. He was a teenaged boy and lack of control was a normal part of the package.

This was going to be a complete and total nightmare.

The Censoring of the Word Shifter

It has become increasingly clear that the Human-Proofing Committee (HPC) of Shifterville has its work cut out for it. These brave men and women have been tasked with ensuring our town is completely human ready by August 1. This has given them a mere three months to whip this town and its residents into shape.

The problems are many and the solutions too few as they strive to ensure that all the public buildings in town are human friendly. Perhaps the most egregious result of these efforts is their intention to remove the word "shifter" from all our public buildings and publications.

As I'm sure our readers can imagine, this came as quite a shock to all the employees of this newspaper. In fact, though we did our best to achieve an exception to this ruling so that we might maintain our highly regarded and noble name, *The Daily Shifter,* we were ultimately unsuccessful. As a result, this will be the final edition of this publication under that name. Moving forward, this paper will be published under the exceedingly normal and ridiculously human name of *The Shifferville Times.*

Do not despair though. We will continue to play homage to the name *The Daily Shifter* until August 1 of this year, at which point, that name shall be no more.

This is perhaps the most devastating change this town is having to undergo – the renaming of our beloved town and its venerable institutions. Many business owners have expressed their displeasure with this change in a variety of clever ways. Members of the HPC have found it increasingly difficult to be served at The Shifter Diner and the Shifter Ice Cream Parlor (henceforth, known under the name of Shiffer). They've also found the bank is closed when they need to make a withdrawal or that the bookstore no longer stocks their favorite authors.

Unfair? Perhaps. Especially since the residents of the town did vote in favor of these changes. However, the reality of what they've let themselves in for is just beginning to settle in.

At the end of the day, it isn't that we've had to change our names. It's that we've had to strike from our very lexicon a word that truly encapsulates our identity as a people: SHIFTER.

Norris Raccoon is a reporter for *The Daily Shifter.*

Human-Proofing the Menus of ~~Shifterville~~ Shifferville

Well the Human-Proofing Committee (HPC) is at it again. There was quite a ruckus at the ~~Shifter Cafe~~ Shiffer Cafe this morning as the HPC attempted to humanize the cafe's menu. Apparently, though this menu has been in place at the cafe for decades, it isn't even a little human-friendly.

The owners, Max Grizzly and Stella Flamingo, were appalled at the suggestion that they would have to completely re-write their menu. "Does that mean we have to come up with human foods to serve?" Flamingo demanded. "There's simply no way. We're a shifter establishment!"

Her husband Grizzly agreed. "We'll just hide away the menus and serve whatever they ask for. Hopefully we'll know how to make it." The HPC tried to insist, but apparently quailed in the face of Grizzly's wrath.

The scene at the cafe, however, was nothing compared to the shouting that occurred at the Shiffer Ice Cream Parlor later that afternoon when the HPC attempted to have acorn ice cream removed from the menu.

Melissa Siamese, owner of the parlor, was quoted as saying, "I would never remove any of the popular ice creams from our menu. Acorn Crunch is a highly profitable flavor, a personal favorite of our porcupine and squirrel populations. Why there would be a riot if I removed it from the menu!"

When the HPC next suggested the removal of tuna ice cream, Siamese exploded. "Humans eat tuna! Why on earth would I remove such a beloved flavor? Why, it's my own personal favorite! Our menu is perfect, just the way it is!"

The HPC was reportedly stymied in the face of such sheer implacability. At this point, the likelihood of this town being ready for the humans' arrival is in serious doubt.

Norris Raccoon is a reporter for *The Shifferville Times* (formerly known as *The Daily Shifter*).

Human-Proofing ~~Shifter High~~ Shiffer High

Moving through the chaos of construction at Shiffer High, it's increasingly clear that the school has the greatest burden of all the buildings in ~~Shifterville~~ Shifferville, in terms of preparing for our newest human arrivals. Bad enough that the only applicant for our veterinarian position is a human, but for him to have a teenaged daughter is an absolute disaster for Shiffer High and its principal, Steve Armadillo.

Armadillo has had to empty out the prized trophy case in the school's main hall, removing his own championship trophy for claw put. All the other school awards, including its ten pawball championships, seventeen 100-yard burrow medals, and twenty wrestling (predator and prey class) trophies are no longer displayed in the great hall of Shiffer High. When asked what will replace these items in the case, Armadillo simply replied, "Something human, no doubt."

The cafeterias are also undergoing a transformation. No longer labeled herbivore, carnivore and omnivore, these cafeterias will now be known by the generic titles of A, B, C and so forth. Let's hope incoming freshmen don't become confused. No herbivore wants to be trapped in a cafeteria full of hungry carnivores.

The art classroom no longer has art displaying shifters in mid-transformation. The music room's shifter songbooks have been locked into a storage closet, no doubt to be replaced with more human-friendly songs. No more school chant about the triumphs of all species working together. No more predators vs. prey songs for Halloween. No more *Shifter Clans Gone By* to ring in the New Year. It is truly a sad day for Shifferville and its teenaged residents.

While the high school is being human-proofed as swiftly as possible, it is obvious Principal Armadillo has quite the challenge in front of him. When asked what his plans were for the school crest, with its human silhouette morphing into those of a turaco bird, a jaguar and a hedgehog, Armadillo simply threw up his hands and shouted, "Do I look like a miracle worker?" and stormed off.

One thing is for certain. Armadillo *will* need to work miracles this summer if he intends to keep his newest student, the human named Amelia, from discovering the truth of Shifferville and its residents.

Norris Raccoon is a reporter for *The Shifferville Times* (formerly known as *The Daily Shifter*).

The Rack of Destruction

It's no secret in this community that the greatest danger to all shifters everywhere is the possibility of humans discovering our existence. For centuries, we have protected this information, guarded our secret and kept the humans in the dark. Now, for the first time in Shifferville history, two humans will be living in our town.

Despite dire predictions and against insurmountable odds, the town is ready for the humans' arrival next week. Indeed, even our esteemed high school principal, Steve Armadillo, managed to perform miracles this summer. The entire town, high school included, has been human-proofed.

This being the case, we should expect to be able to breathe a sigh of relief. Instead, tensions mount as one teen demonstrates again and again that he is unable to control his unruly rack. Attempts to interview Melvin Moose have failed, as he swiftly ran in the opposite direction anytime he was approached. Other residents of Shifferville have much to say, however.

"He just can't control that ridiculous rack," Laney Siamese, a classmate of Melvin's, complained.

"It seems every time I turn around, there's Melvin, knocking over something or someone. I mean, how hard is it to just stay human, for heaven's sake?"

"He's going to be the end of us all," Cora Jaguar, owner of Shiffer Grocery predicted.

Bets are already being placed around town, with odds of 1,000 to one in favor of Melvin's antlers revealing our secret. Other possibilities were suggested, including the presence of tuna-flavored ice cream at the parlor in town (as previously reported, Melissa Siamese refused to remove it, insisting that humans eat tuna too) and the decision to allow students to continue dressing out in fur in P.E. Of course, these suggestions came from Melvin Moose's best friend, Paulie Porcupine, and Melvin's father, Jacob Moose, both of whom appear to be in the minority when it comes to predicting how long our secret will be safe with Melvin's rack on the loose.

Overall, the opinion of the town is clear: Melvin Moose's rack has the highest probability of destroying the secret shifters have guarded for centuries. Buckle up, Shifferville, it's going to be a rocky ride!

Norris Raccoon is a reporter for *The Shifferville Times.*

THE TROUBLE WITH ANTLERS (a.k.a. Melvin's Rampant Rack)

SH

Shifter High: Season 1, Episode 1

Written By
A.J. CULEY

contents

the applicant

THE VETERINARIAN'S NAME was George Finch. His Skype interview didn't exactly go smoothly.

"Would you show us your animal?" the town's mayor, David Peacock asked.

"Uh, sure," George replied. "Which one though? I have a lot of animals."

"You do?" the mayor exclaimed.

"Why, yes. I have three cats, one dog, five rabbits and a chinchilla."

Silence.

"No … finches?"

George laughed. "Uh, no. I've never actually had a pet bird, despite the last name."

"Pet – but – " Silence. The mayor and George stared at each other from across the nation. This was becoming the weirdest Skype conversation either one had ever experienced.

"Well, um, we do like to invite all of our employees to dress out, you know." The mayor coughed delicately. "We want you to feel comfortable in our town. We'd be happy to dress out too."

"Um. Dress out?"

"In your natural form."

"Wait a minute." George squirmed uncomfortably and squinted at the iPad. "Is this an interview for a *nudist* colony?"

The mayor blinked. And then he blinked again. And then the truth dawned on him. Was he interviewing a *human*?

The mayor quickly terminated the interview, with a promise to let George know the outcome as soon as possible. He then demanded his assistant do a bit more research on this George Finch.

The results were emphatic and undeniable.

George Finch, despite his unlikely name, was a human.

Town Council Meeting, three days later

"Here's the thing," David said. He'd just spent the past fifteen minutes describing his interview with George Finch to the council. "He's our only applicant."

"But he's a human! We can't have humans in our town," Steve Armadillo, the school's principal protested.

"What about the other shifter towns? No one has a single veterinarian looking for work?" Margaret Fox asked.

"None," David said glumly. "I've emailed and Muzzlebooked the mayor of every single town in the U.S. and Canada and nothing."

"What about Tweeter?" Jessica Canary demanded. "Not all birds are on Muzzlebook, you know."

"Jessica, I'm a peacock. Of course I feather-well tweeted. No one replied. Not one single shifter. Bird, mammal, reptile, I tried them all."

"Fumblr?" Joseph Grizzly asked.

"Posted pictures, videos, even a flared-up infomercial about our town and the position. Nothing."

"Well, we need a vet," Steve said. "We can't keep asking Murdock Mallard to treat our animal ailments."

"I don't see why not," Joseph said. "He's a doctor, ain't he?"

"Yes, but he studied human ailments, not animal ones. He threatened to quit last week." David sighed.

"What? We can't lose our only other doctor." Steve jumped to his feet. "David, we've got to do something."

David nodded. "That's why we're here. We really don't have a choice, shifters. Either we open our town to this human or we risk losing Murdock too."

"It's all Hardy's fault," Joseph growled. "Dung whiny giraffe. So what if he got a crick in his neck? Where's the loyalty, I ask you."

"Hardy turned 93 last month," David said. "Don't you think he deserved to retire?"

"Not to Africa! He could have stuck around until we found someone, couldn't he?"

"He did stick around.   He handed in his resignation three hacking years ago."

"Three years?" Joe looked around at the others. "Has it really been three years?"

"Ninetieth birthday party," Jessica said. "He announced his retirement then."

"Besides, it wasn't really Hardy's fault," Margaret said. "It was the rodents' fault."

"Oh, lord, not this again, Maggie." David groaned.

"I'm just saying. Those rodents are always causing trouble. Between the moles digging holes and the rabbits eating everyone's vegetables, it's a wonder Hardy lasted as long as he did."

"Rabbits aren't rodents, Maggie, they're lagomorphs," David said.

"Whatever.   The point is they're small and they're pests and they caused Hardy to move away."

"How in the world do you figure that, Maggie?" Steve asked.

"He got a crick in his neck, didn't he? No doubt from bending over all those dang rodents and tiny critters all day."

"Don't be ridiculous, Mags," Joe said.

"Ridiculous? It's not ridiculous to - "

"Enough!" David slammed his hands to the table. "It doesn't matter who's at fault, we're stuck with this situation and we have to come to a decision. Now. What are the chances of our being able to hide our secret if we invite this human to town?   Seriously. What are the chances?"

"Well," Jessica hesitated. "We could move him into a house on the outskirts of town, keep him as far from the center of town as possible."

"We'd have to change the names of pretty much every furbegotten building," Joe said. "Something simple. Maybe change the 't' to an 'f'. That'd work. Instead of Shifterville, we'd become Shifferville. We're not on any human maps, so there's no danger there."

David nodded. "Okay, that's good. What else?"

"We'd have to institute new rules about shifting. No more paw-slippers or eyeglasses for our shifter forms," Steve said.

"Um, I think we have a bigger problem than just the human male," Jessica said, staring down at her iPhone.

"What's wrong?" David asked.

"George Finch, you said?"

"Yeah."

"Lives in New York?"

"Yeah."

"Only veterinarian in New York with that name has a fifteen-year old daughter. Her name's Amelia." Jessica turned her phone to show the Council a picture of a smiling teen. "Cute, yeah?"

"No, no, no, no, no," Steve said. "Absolutely not. We cannot have a human girl roaming around my high school. No, David. Absolutely not. There's no way we can keep something this big from her. Think of the cafeteria lines alone. It'd be impossible. Shrubs, acorns, raw meats, bamboo shoots. No way. No way we can do this."

"Calm down, Steve," David said. "You have plenty of cafeterias. Just set it up so she eats in the one with more ... human foods."

"What about our curriculum? History of Shifters? Wildlife Education? Shifter Anatomy?"

"You already do a split day, with human classes half the time and shifter ones the other half. Set her up with some independent study classes instead of the shifter ones."

"Do you have any idea how difficult it is to get a functioning, reasonable schedule in place in time for school each year? Throwing a human in the mix is going to make everything disastrously more complicated!"

David sighed. "We'll delay their arrival until right before school starts. Surely we can manage three more months without a vet. That'll give us the entire summer to get things set up, to prep the town and the kids."

Steve shook his head. "You do understand the high school's just a hotbed of hormones waiting to explode?"

"You're an excellent principal, Steve," Jessica said. "Surely you can handle anything that comes up."

"Normally, yes, but shifter hormones. Boy shifter hormones. Around a human who smells like prey."

"Not to all of them," Jessica said. "Many are vegetarians. Just try to arrange the schedule so she's not with that many predators."

"Are you kidding me? Too many of our prey families have

moved away, something about living with predators being bad for their emotional health."

"What's your point?" David glowered.

"My point is that predators in the school now outnumber prey three to one! It's all I can do to protect our rabbit-shifters and mole-shifters. Now you want me to protect a human too?"

"That's not going to be your biggest problem, Steve," Joe said, letting out a bark of laughter.

"What are you talking about?"

"It's not a what, but a who."

"Who, then?" Steve glowered at him.

Joe grinned. "Melvin Moose."

"Oh, dear," Maggie whispered.

"Melvin," Jessica murmured.

"Oh for shift's sake," Steve said, "what am I supposed to do about Melvin?"

moose meets girl

MELVIN WAS LATE for gym class. Again. Life kind of sucked lately. Ever since he hit puberty and his antlers grew in, they were a huge load to bear. Literally. They'd already popped out twice this morning, once when Laney *Queen-of-the-Universe* Siamese gave him that haughty look and tossed her hair over her shoulders.

It wasn't his fault! Her silky hair brushed his nose and he got a headful of heady girl-cat scent and out they sprang.

Boing!

All the kids in the hallway laughed (except the two he knocked down with his headful of dorkiness... and the other two kids he flattened when his antlers pulled him to the ground in yet another example of gravity working against him).

The second time was when sweet, little Kelly Mole blinked up at him from her book as he walked by her in English class. She was a naked mole rat for heaven's sake, but did his antlers care? Of course not! They were moose antlers and they sensed girl and that was all it took.

Mrs. Saber snarled at him to get his rack under control and that sent the entire room into gales of laughter.

It had taken him ten minutes in the bathroom to will those antlers into submission and now he was late for gym, where he'd be forced to dress out in fur, thus giving those antlers free reign again.

Barreling down the hall, internally ranting at the horrors of his antlerhood, Melvin never even scented the new girl, the *human*, coming around the corner.

Every single adult in school had taken the time to lecture him about avoiding the new girl.

One glimpse of his antlers and the secret of their shifter town, a secret their town had guarded for centuries, was toast. But he wasn't thinking about that. He was worried about being late and cursing his antlers as he barreled around the corner.

He caught a glimpse of bright blue eyes and then their bodies slammed together in a tangle of arms and legs. He reflexively caught her in his arms, her scent barreled over him and BAM! Out sprang the antlers of doom.

The only good news?

They knocked New Girl out with one blow, sending her unconscious to the floor, possibly ensuring she never knew what hit her, possibly ensuring the town's secret was safe.

Melvin leaned forward to check on her and - yikes!

His antlers and gravity toppled him over.

He flung out his arms to catch his fall and ended up crouched over her body.

This wasn't good.

Should he just leave her there, unconscious on the floor?

He placed two fingers against her neck, where her pulse should be. Except - she was fully human. Would that change the location of her pulse? He tried to remember what he'd learned in his human anatomy class, but her scent was so distracting.

She smelled divine.

Not because he thought she'd be tasty - he was a vegetarian, for goodness' sake, but something else. Something amazing. He grabbed his rack to keep it from becoming fresh with the human and leaned forward to take a big whiff.

The girl's eyes opened.

"Hi," Melvin said.

She groaned, rolled to her side, placed a hand on the floor and wobbled as she tried to get to her knees. "What happened?"

Melvin didn't answer. He jumped up, desperate to hide his antlers. The teachers would kill him if she –

The girl staggered to her feet, turned, caught sight of his antlers and went down again.

Melvin tried to catch her, but he was afraid of impaling her on his rack and moved too slowly as a result.

She was out cold *again*.

Melvin knelt, this time tilting his head back to keep from overbalancing. He slid his arms beneath the girl, lifted her and stood. Now what?

He cradled her against his chest. Her long, black hair brushed against his ear and she sighed against his neck, her breath tickling his chin.

If his antlers weren't already unruly and out, that would have done it.

There was no hope for it. He was going to have to carry her to the nurse's office.

He set off down the hall. He walked past the cafeteria where study hall was.

He heard whispers begin inside the room and cringed. Had they seen him? He walked past the next door and an explosion of sound came from inside.

They'd *definitely* seen him.

"Melvin Moose!" Mrs. Crane squawked from behind him.

Melvin faced the study hall teacher.

She stood in the cafeteria door and her students crowded behind her, trying to see.

"Yes, Mrs. Crane?"

"What are you doing with that girl?"

"She fainted, Mrs. Crane."

"Your antlers are out. She didn't see them, did she?"

Melvin hesitated.

"You have got to be kidding me. It's only her first day in this school and you've already revealed the secret this town has spent centuries protecting. You weren't even supposed to be near that girl."

"I don't think she got a good look."

"Oh, I suppose she just fainted at the sight of your face?"

"Well, see, I came around the corner and I didn't see her. We ran into each other and my antlers popped out and they knocked her out." Melvin rushed through the last of his explanation, running all the words together.

"They knocked her out?" Mrs. Crane repeated incredulously.

Snickers broke out among the students.

She whirled on them. "Get back to your seats right now. Study, study, study."

The students edged away and slowly walked back to their seats.

Mrs. Crane waited until every student was seated, then she faced him again. "Well, what are you doing with her?"

"I was taking her to the nurse."

"And do you think that's a good idea, young man?"

"Umm."

"The *girl* is *human*. You were to avoid all contact with her and now she's *seen* you. And to make matters worse, you're carrying her through the school! What if she wakes again and sees you?"

"Well—"

"Give her to me. Now."

Melvin passed the girl to Mrs. Crane.

"I'll see she gets to the nurse. You get to class, young man."

"Yes, ma'am." Melvin walked away.

"And control that rack!"

three

gangs

AMELIA PULLED OPEN the door and slipped inside. The endless stacks of books instantly comforted. She was there to hide from the other students. There was just no other way to say it – the teachers were scary, but the students were downright terrifying.

Every last one of them.

When she'd shown up for P.E., the teacher had refused to let her inside.

"What are you doing here?" he'd demanded, blocking the door. He was so huge, he filled the doorframe from top to bottom and side to side.

"Uh… my schedule says I have gym."

"I'm late, I'm late, I'm late," a voice squeaked behind her. Turning, Amelia saw a small boy racing toward her. Could he possibly be a high schooler? He was seriously only three feet tall.

He darted around her and barreled into the mammoth teacher blocking the doorway. With a squeal of horror, the kid bounced back toward Amelia, who just barely managed to jump out of the way.

"You!" the mammoth roared.   "In the locker room now!
Dress out this instant, you puny little mole. Naked, now!"

Amelia's eyes widened. "I ... what? They have to play naked?"
No freaking way was she going to engage in any naked sports. No
way, no how.

"Don't be absurd!" the teacher snapped. "They dress out in ff-
clothes, just like everyone else."

Ff-clothes?

"Go to the office now," he told her.

"But – I – gym?"

"You don't need gym. Just go to the office and tell them to
sign you up for art or music or something else that doesn't involve
fff-dressing out!"

So Amelia headed for the office, but something must have
happened because the next thing she knew, she was lying down in
the nurse's office with an ice pack on her head and a new schedule
clutched in her hand.

Nurse Polar had fussed over her a bit, then sent her to class
where the girl to her left called her a freaky little human two
seconds before the guy behind her leaned forward and *sniffed* her
hair.

She turned and demanded, "Did you just sniff me?"

He had the weirdest dye job she'd ever seen: spiky yellow hair
with splotches of brown in it. His eyes matched his hair (who
wore contacts to match their hair?) and he smiled. It wasn't a nice

smile.

"I did," he said.

He didn't even deny it! "Why?"

"You smell like –" He stopped.

"Like what?" Amelia demanded.

"Prey."

And she was done. "Pervert." Amelia stood, grabbed her bookbag and stalked out of class.

It'd just been the very last straw in a really long and disturbing day.

So now here she was inside the library, trying to forget the kids who had driven her there.

They had to be gang members. An entire school full of gangs. Maybe her dad would agree to move back home if she told him about the freaky boy who sniffed her hair in calculus.

She slipped between the stacks of books and headed deeper into the library. It was quiet and smelled just right. Books and more books. She turned a corner and found a small alcove with a couple armchairs and a table. A big burly guy sat in one of the chairs. His long legs were stretched out in front of him and his head was resting on the back of the chair.

She had a weird feeling his eyes would be brown.

The guy's eyes opened and she was right. He focused on her and his entire body jerked. He slammed both hands to his head and let out a weird-sounding grunt.

Great. Not just gang members, but the socially awkward as

well.

Rolling her eyes, Amelia turned and stalked off down another aisle.

A loud clatter sounded behind her. Something heavy had fallen, maybe onto the table or the floor. Whatever. She didn't care. She just wanted to find a quiet corner to wait out the rest of the day.

No more freaks today!

four

the bookbag

"HOW WAS YOUR day, kiddo?" Amelia's dad asked as he pulled out of the school's parking lot.

"Sucked." Amelia couldn't wait to get home so she could go for a walk in the woods and get away from everything and everyone.

"Oh, it couldn't have been that bad. Surely you made at least one friend?"

"Not even close," Amelia muttered.

"Well, give it time."

"I don't want to give it time, Dad. I don't know why we had to move. Seriously. Can't we just go back to New York?"

"Not a chance. This is a new start for us, Amelia. Just give it a shot. Things'll get better."

"Whatever."

"You like their pets."

"Yeah, but they're not normal pets."

"Just because I haven't treated any cats or dogs yet –"

"Haven't seen any either. I mean, what kind of freaks have wildcats and raccoons for pets? Is that even legal?"

"The entire town's a wildlife refuge. It's one of the reasons I took the job. Figured you'd think it was cool."

"Well, sure, the animals are cool, but —"

"See there? Amazing!"

Up ahead, a giant moose walked along the side of the road.

Weird. Was that a bookbag hanging from its antlers? Amelia stared as they passed by.

It *was* a bookbag and it had an ornament, an animal of some sort, hanging from the strap.

Amelia swiveled in her seat to keep the moose in sight, but in the time it took her to turn around, the bookbag had disappeared, the moose's antlers unadorned.

Great.

Now she was seeing things.

Melvin stared down into the ditch. He'd jerked his head to the side when the car smelling of humans had passed by. His bag had gone flying and now lay at the bottom of the ditch. Like his life wasn't complicated enough.

He should have waited until he got home to let his beast out, but he'd been desperate by the end of the day. His moose wasn't waiting a second longer than the ringing of that final bell. He'd raced for the locker rooms and barely managed to tear off his clothes and shove them into his bag before everything went moose-sized.

Now he was halfway home and his bookbag with his geometry homework and history assignment were somewhere down below. Not to mention his clothes. Of course, with his terrible moose vision, he couldn't see a thing.

He paced back and forth at the top of the ditch, tilting his head this way and that, trying to catch a glimpse of his bag, but he just couldn't see past the end of his snout.

His front legs were longer than his back, which would help him jump over this ditch, but not necessarily navigate his way down it. The ditch was simply too steep and his moose-form too lacking in grace.

He let out a bellow of frustration.

He turned in a circle. There was no one around. He sniffed the air. No humans nearby. No shifters either.

Melvin closed his eyes and focused on his human form.

A cracking sound echoed as his bones broke and shrank, refitting themselves to his still rather-large human form.

Melvin's knees buckled and gravity did the rest. He landed facedown in the mud at the bottom of the ditch.

Good news was he landed on his bookbag.

Melvin struggled to his feet and yanked the bag out of the mud.

He looked down at himself.

Naked.

Covered in mud.

Awesome.

He tried to shift back to his moose form, dreading how the mud would become trapped in uncomfortable places. Nothing happened though.

He tried again, then let out a second bellow, his voice cracking mid-shout, so that he sounded like a moose-human hybrid experiment gone awry.

Shifting drained energy, making each subsequent shift harder to achieve. Full-grown shifters could manage four or even five full shifts in a 24-hour period, but that took years of practice and control.

The little control Melvin had gained over the years had been obliterated when his moose-orrific antlers came in. With those involuntary partial shifts happening pretty much every time he turned around, he had no control whatsoever. And since he'd already partially shifted multiple times today and fully shifted twice, once this morning and once just now, he was pretty much out of luck.

Fantastic.

He'd spent the entire day trying to avoid the shift and now that he *needed* it, nothing.

He pulled the zipper of his bag, but it didn't move.

This was not happening.

He needed clothes or his moose form now.

He shook the bag furiously, then jerked on the zipper again. The movement caused him to slip and he landed on his rump in the mud. Muttering a curse word, he struggled to his feet. Forget the jeans.

He popped his head above the ditch and looked around. Still clear.

He swung the bag onto his shoulder and leapt to the top of the ditch, then took off across a field, headed for the woods that ran the length of town.

Amelia jumped down from the back porch and walked across the yard into the woods behind her house.

Her dad had dropped her off, but almost immediately left again, responding to a call for vet services. Normally Amelia would go with him. She loved meeting new animals and helping her dad care for them, but today she just wanted to be left alone.

All she'd wanted was one friend. It shouldn't be that difficult. She'd been at enough schools to know that making at least one friend was easy, if she just set her mind to it. But this town wasn't like the others and the kids were in a class of their own.

Her dad never liked to stay in one place for too long. He'd hire on at a vet's office, stay there for a year or even two and then he'd get restless and start looking for a new place to land. It made her crazy, having to switch schools all the time, though she did like the adventure of it occasionally. This time, though, he'd promised to try to stay at least until she graduated from high school. Four more years. Surely he could handle four years. That's what she'd thought anyway.

But then they'd landed here. In Freakville. And now she was the one who balked at the thought of four years.

Melvin reached the shallow stream, dropped his bag on the bank and plowed into the freezing cold water. He leaned over, scooped water into his hands and scrubbed at the mud hardening on his skin. Itchy.

He scrubbed harder, dislodging mud from all kinds of hideous places.

A gasp sounded from the bank.

He whirled.

New Girl stood at the edge of the stream, staring at him with wide eyes.

Seriously? Could he never catch a break?

He lunged for his bag, scooped it up and held it strategically in front of him. "Do you mind?"

"Mind? You're the one who's naked in the middle of the woods! Anyone could come along and see you. Someone did, in fact. Me! What's wrong with you?" New Girl, cheeks flaming red, whirled so her back was to Melvin. "Well go on, get dressed."

Melvin fiddled with the zipper some more, but it still wouldn't open. "No can do."

"What? Why not?"

"Zipper's stuck."

"Let me see." She held out a hand behind her.

Melvin hesitated. Was there anything inside the bookbag she

shouldn't see? He wasn't sure.

"Well, come on!"

Melvin tossed it her way.

New Girl scooped it up, jiggled with the zipper a few minutes, then slung the open bag back to him.

Melvin glowered at her back. Seriously, how had she done that?

He jerked his jeans out and slung the bag onto the bank. "Bullwinkle," he muttered, attempting to force his soaking wet legs into the tight, restrictive jeans. Hopping around, he stumbled on a rock and almost face planted again.

Growling, he dragged the jeans off, flung them onto the bank, and pulled his boxers out of the bag.

For the love of horns.

Why *these* boxers?

Of all days to have a laundry crisis.

Gritting his teeth, he pulled on the bright red shorts and decided to make *her* leave first.

"Well?" New Girl demanded. "Are you decent?"

"More or less." He pulled on his t-shirt, then settled his glasses on his nose.

Much better. Now he could see in detail the incredulous look on New Girl's face when she turned and stared at him.

That's when he realized his antlers were behaving themselves for once. He rubbed his head, marveling at the lack of itching. There was no tingling, no stretching sensation that signaled an impending partial shift. Was he finally cured of his terminally rampant rack?

Unlikely.

Instead, because he'd shifted so much today, the ability was likely lost to him until tomorrow.

Sweet. Glorious. Freedom.

"Hello? Freak-Boy?"

"Huh?"

"What's your name?" The way she said it, drawing out her words, made him think it wasn't the first time she'd asked.

"Oh, uh, Melvin. You?"

"Amelia. Why were you naked, Melvin?"

"Uh, I like skinny-dipping."

"In a stream?" Amelia asked. "It's not like you can swim in there."

"Well, I like it," Melvin said. It was a ridiculous response, he knew, but he wasn't very good at making up stories on the fly and this girl – Amelia – was seriously starting to annoy him. What business was it of hers if he liked to wander naked through the woods? She'd probably shut up real fast if he showed her his moose.

"Wasn't it cold?"

Melvin shrugged.

Amelia leaned over and tested the water. "It's not cold. It's freezing! Are you insane?"

"Probably."

"Well, that's cool, I guess. So what do you do for fun around here?"

"Fun?"

"Yeah. Fun."

Melvin had to think about that. What did they do for fun?

They shifted.

"Well, we sometimes hang out –" He hesitated. Where could he tell her the kids hung out where he knew not one of them would be in shifter form? "Um, there's an all-you-can-eat buffet." Wait. The buffet probably wasn't safe either since it sold bamboo shoots for the pandas, raw meat for the carnivores and shrubs for moose like him. Dewlap-licious.

"An all-you-can-eat buffet?"

The look on Amelia's face told Melvin she wasn't bowled over by the buffet option. "Well, we also have a bowling alley" (that was probably safe), "an arcade," (also safe), "and an outdoor arena for all types of sports" (not so safe, shouldn't have mentioned that one).

Amelia made a face. "I'm not much into sports."

Thank goodness.

"And I pretty much suck at bowling. No clubs?"

"One, but it's only open on the weekends and you have to be 21 to get in." That was a lie. There was a 21 and older club, but it was in the city. The club in Shifterville was a teen hangout, but their secret would be out the minute she walked in the door.

Why had the town council thought this was a good idea?

There was no way these humans could live here and not learn their secret. Unless they were stupid.

Melvin eyed Amelia. She didn't look stupid.

"So basically, there's nothing to do around here," she said.

"Pretty much."

"Awesome. I don't know why my dad had to choose this town."

"You could always leave."

Amelia snorted. "Yeah, tell that to my dad."

"Well, I should get going." Before he got roped into showing her around or something. Everyone would freak out if they saw them together. Melvin grabbed his bookbag and slung it over his shoulder. "Nice to meet you, Amelia."

"Yeah, you too."

Amelia's eyes widened as Melvin walked away.

What. The. Helvetica.

Across the backspace of his red boxers, in bold white letters, were the words "gluteus maxi-moose."

five

the count

ON THE DRIVE to school the next day, Amelia's dad gave her a pep talk about making friends and how this wasn't that different from every other town they'd lived in over the years.

Just an ordinary town, Amelia thought. *Yeah, right.*

Her dad droned on in the background about how Amelia always managed to make at least one friend in the first couple days of school, didn't she? And how he just knew she'd make a ton of friends in no time, blah-blah-blah-blah-blah.

Because Amelia really wanted to be friends with a bunch of people who acted as feral as the animals they adopted.

"Right, Amelia?"

"Sure, but come on, Dad. Don't you think it's weird they all have animal last names?"

"Well, honey, our last name's Finch."

"Not the same, Dad."

"I suppose not, but honestly, I think it's pretty awesome that everyone in this town has adopted an animal. I told you, Amelia, the entire town's committed to saving endangered species."

"I don't think the Siamese cat is an endangered species, Dad."

"What?"

"This girl in my calculus class – her name's Laney Siamese."

Her dad smiled. "That's pretty cool, don't you think? She obviously loves cats."

"Whatever." Why couldn't her dad see how weird this town was, how weird its people were? Of course, he did spend all his time with animals. These people probably felt more familiar to him than normal people. Ugh.

Thankfully they arrived at the school and Amelia was able to escape her father's continued lecture about making friends with freaks and such.

The morning was mostly uneventful. Amelia avoided talking. She also avoided making eye contact. She simply sat back and listened. And what she heard was just weird.

First of all, how often did people actually use the word *human* in their everyday conversations? Because even though she never quite heard exactly what was being said, she'd heard that word fourteen times by lunch.

Fifteen times.

She was starting to think crazy things. Like vampires. Or aliens. She tried to reign her imagination, but the people around her just kept adding to her suspicions.

She hadn't really noticed the day before, but apparently the entire school ate at the exact same time (no staggered lunches like in other schools she'd attended), but they didn't eat in the same places. She'd watched and listened and from what she could tell, there were at least three cafeterias somewhere in the school, maybe even more. She didn't really know where the others were, but she was definitely prohibited from exploring.

For the second day in a row, her English teacher, Mrs. Saber, latched onto Amelia's arm and led her to one specific cafeteria. "This cafeteria is yours," she reminded Amelia. "You're not allowed in any other cafeteria. Always this one. Cafeteria A."

Amelia nodded. "Okay." It wasn't okay. It was weird. As always. Just weird. She needed to find a new word. A new word to describe this town, this school, these people. For now, though, they were just weird.

Stepping into the cafeteria was like stepping into a different world. The chaos of the hallways – the noise and the movement – just died away as the door closed behind Amelia. The calm and quiet was eerie, almost like a library. The kids already seated were eating quietly, focused on their food, the silence occasionally broken by the soft murmur of conversation. The students in line were standing quietly, most of them not speaking, just … bouncing.

Amelia raised a brow and stepped to the side of the line to get a better view. It was true. They were all bouncing. Some of them just seemed to sway a bit, rolling from their feet flat on the floor to balancing on the balls of their feet, then back again. Others, like the girl in front of Amelia, were actually hopping, their feet leaving the ground again and again, in a series of rhythmic bounces.

As if the girl sensed Amelia staring, she bounced around to face her, light brown pigtails flying in an arc with the movement. "Hi! My name's Felicia!" She hopped backward as the line moved forward. Bounce-bounce-bounce. "Are you the hu–new girl?"

"Um, yeah. My name's Amelia."

"Awesome!" Bounce-bounce-bounce. "I love it when we get new students!" Bounce-bounce-bounce. "How do you like our school so far?" Bounce-bounce.

"It's," Amelia hesitated, "interesting."

"Oh, definitely! We're super-interesting!" Felicia stopped bouncing, but now her toes were patting the ground in a rhythmic thumping. "What classes are you in?" Patter-patter-patter. "What do you like to do after school?" Thump-Thump. "Do you play any sports?" With this question, Felicia began to bounce again.

"Um. Well, I'm taking art and computer programming and – careful!" Amelia reached out a hand as Felicia almost bounced into the stack of plates at the start of the food line.

"Oh!" Felicia giggled and turning, hopped forward, grabbed a plate, then whirled back around, all the while jumping in place, "So art. I love art. Maybe we're in class together."

"I, um, maybe." Amelia couldn't remember seeing Felicia in her art class earlier that morning, but she'd been focused on avoiding attention and not speaking.

"I'm in 2nd hour, with Mrs. Spider, of course, because she's the only art teacher after what happened last year with–" The entire time she was speaking, Felicia was bouncing, bouncing, bouncing, until all of a sudden, on that last word, she landed, her eyes widened and she turned away, no more bounce in her step.

"What happened last year?" Amelia asked.

"Oh, nothing. Don't mind me, just being silly." Felicia began filling her plate with veggies.

More secrets. Amelia huffed, grabbed a plate and began to build a salad. "I think you might be right. I have history first hour, then art next, so we're probably in the same class. Sorry I didn't recognize–"

"Oh, that's okay." Felicia started to hop again, as she moved down the line, piling more and more veggies on her tray.

"Um, do you want another plate?"

"Nope." Bounce-bounce-pile of radishes-bounce. "I'm fine." Hop-hop-scoop-of-parsley-hop.

"Is that parsley?" Amelia asked, leaning forward.

"Oh, yes, I love parsley, don't you? And cilantro!" Jump-jump, scoop of cilantro.

Amelia had never seen anyone pile so many vegetables together on one plate before. Or tray. Whatever. It was a little astonishing. Then she noticed the guy behind her had two trays, each piled high with at least twice as many vegetables as Felicia had. "Whoa."

"Is that all you're going to eat?"

Amelia looked down at her tray. Her salad wasn't even half finished. "Um, no, no, I need–" She scanned the salad bar. Not that. Or that. And definitely none of that. Breathing a sigh of relief when she finally saw some traditional salad toppings, she scooped up some cucumbers, tomatoes and sprinkled cheese on top of everything.

She reached the end of the aisle and perused their salad dressing options. The usual suspects. Ranch, French, Italian, Thousand Island. She hesitated, then chose ranch, carefully dribbling it over the entire salad. She put the ladle back and it was then that she realized the cafeteria, which she'd thought was silent before, had suddenly fallen into complete stillness. The shuffle of feet as the kids in line bounced, the clinking of silverware and pots from the kitchen, the soft murmurs of conversation – all of it had stopped.

Slowly lifting her head, Amelia glanced around and realized that everyone was staring at her. Everyone. The kids at the tables. The kids in line. The cafeteria workers. Felicia.

Looking down at her tray, Amelia couldn't see anything wrong. Sure she hadn't filled her tray like Felicia, but she hadn't done anything weird.

"So!" Felicia bounced at her side. "Let's go sit down, okay?" Hop-hop-hop. "You can sit with me!" Patter-patter-patter.

"Okay." Amelia picked up her tray and slowly turned to face the cafeteria.

As if that were a pre-arranged signal, all the students turned away and began to eat again, the soft murmur of conversations once more beginning.

As she followed Felicia to a table, Amelia heard the soft shuffle of feet as they began to bounce once more.

Once they were seated, Felicia introduced Amelia to the others at the table. A whirl of names flew by and Amelia slowly relaxed as everyone at the table greeted her with the same happiness and cheer Felicia had shown her. Once the introductions were done, everyone got back to eating.

Amelia was so busy watching Felicia and the others at her table, she almost forgot to eat her own salad. She was simply amazed at the sight of Felicia eating her way through more vegetables than Amelia probably ate in a week. And Amelia was a vegetarian!

The salad was pretty good, though mostly lacking in protein, which was pretty typical of most school salad bars. She'd have to remember to bring some nuts and maybe an avocado tomorrow.

"So why do you put that stuff on your salad?" Felicia was still bouncing, bopping up and down in her seat, just a little, but as Amelia looked around, she realized the entire room was pretty much a constant wave of motion. Amelia shook her head and closed her eyes. Jeez, dizzy.

"Amelia?" Bounce-bounce-bounce.

"I'm sorry, what?"

"Why'd you put the white stuff on your lunch?"

"The – you mean my salad dressing?"

"Uh-huh!" Patter-patter-patter.

Amelia glanced around, wondering if she was the only one

who'd used the dressings, but apparently everyone had finished eating because their trays were completely clear. Not a single leaf or carrot was in sight.

"Well, it just tastes better, I guess."

"Really?" Felicia's eyes widened. "I can't imagine vegetables tasting any better than they already do!"

"Me neither." A kid across the table from them said and everyone else at the table nodded in agreement.

Had they never tried salad dressing before?

"Wait a minute!" Felicia bounced up out of her chair.

Amelia turned and watched as Felicia hopped all the way to the front of the cafeteria where she spoke to one of the workers there. "What's she doing?"

"Knowing her, getting more veggies," someone answered.

Sure enough, when Felicia turned around, she had a handful of green and orange vegetables in her hand. She bounced back to the table. By the time she reached the table, the entire room had fallen silent again.

Felicia dropped the vegetables onto a couple trays. "Can I try?"

"Try?"

"Your dressing!"

Amelia glanced down at her plate. "Sure." She pushed her tray toward them.

"Oooh, me too!" the kid across from them leaned over and grabbed a piece of lettuce.

Felicia grinned at him. "Okay, Luis. Are you ready?"

"Ready!"

And the two of them swirled their lettuce into the dressing, coating it as much as they could.

"On the count of three," Luis said.

"One," Felicia began, raising her lettuce leaf.

Amelia was getting a bad feeling about this.

"Two," everyone at the table counted.

"Um, maybe—"

"Three!" everyone in the cafeteria roared.

And Luis and Felicia took a huge bite out of their covered lettuce leaves. For a few moments, the only sound in the cafeteria was that of Luis and Felicia chewing.

Then, at almost the exact same moment, they both leaned over and spit the remaining lettuce out.

The rest of the students who had been standing around watching the experiment laughed and wandered back to their seats, whispering to each other.

Amelia only caught a few words, but it was enough for the count to rise fast. *Sixteen-seventeen-eighteen-nineteen.*

Felicia grabbed a napkin and started scrubbing her tongue, wailing, "What was that? What was that?"

Luis was too busy chugging a glass of water to answer her.

"Um, ranch dressing?" Amelia offered.

"It's awful, awful, awful!" With each word, Felicia bounced a little higher. "How can you ruin lettuce? I mean perfectly good lettuce. It's beautiful, divine, delicious. I never knew there was a way to make it so awful!"

"Me neither," gasped Luis, finally having stopped gulping water. "I thought lettuce was perfect, no matter how it was served."

"I need a pepper!" Felicia grabbed an orange one.

"Good idea," Luis agreed and they both started munching.

"I'm so sorry, guys," Amelia said. "I really like ranch dressing. I had no idea you would find it so—"

"Disgusting?" Felicia offered.

"Putrid?" Luis suggested.

"Vile," they chorused together, nodding in agreement.

Amelia couldn't help but laugh. "Yes, I'm so sorry."

The bell rang and suddenly there was a huge rush to toss trash, return trays and get out the doors.

After promising to eat with Felicia and Luis tomorrow, Amelia headed to biology, which was fairly uneventful, mostly because she sat at the back and kept her head down, doodling as the teacher droned on and on about cellular structures.

Finally, biology was over and it was time for computer programming. This would be her first day there, as it was the replacement for P.E., a fantastic turn of events as far as Amelia was concerned, though the programming teacher didn't seem to agree.

"Really?" he snapped when she walked into class. "Are they serious?"

Amelia froze. "Um, sorry?" Everyone was staring at her. She wasn't late. The bell hadn't even rung yet.

"Let me see your schedule. You've got to be in the wrong

place."

"I, uh, I don't think so." Amelia handed him her schedule and watched as he stared down at it. The name on her schedule said Fox, an unlikely name in Amelia's opinion.

Mr. Fox was short and thin, wiry almost, with snow white hair and bushy eyebrows.

He crumpled the paper in his fist. "Unbelievable." His voice was a low rumble, the word almost unrecognizable.

Amelia bit her lip and waited.

Dragging in a deep breath, Mr. Fox slowly turned his head and stared at her. "I suppose they thought this class was the least dangerous for you."

Seriously? Dangerous? Since when was any high school classroom dangerous? Boring maybe. Uncomfortable. Awkward sometimes, but dangerous?

"So, let's find you a seat, a seat, shall we?" A boy grabbed her arm and dragged her past the glowering teacher. "Thanks, Mr. Fox, I'll get her all settled in, all settled in, no worries, no worries, no worries at all."

Amelia couldn't seem to drag her eyes away from Mr. Fox. Even as the boy pulled her past him and turned, dragging her down an aisle full of computers, Amelia kept her eyes on the teacher's, unable to break away.

A hard jerk on her arm caused her to stumble and just like that the spell was broken.

"Stop staring at him. Are you crazy, crazy? Here, sit down, sit down, sit down."

A shove and Amelia was sitting in front of a computer monitor, staring at a blank screen. What had just happened?

The boy settled into the chair next to her. He was so short his feet didn't quite reach the floor and his head just barely reached the top of the monitor. His hair was a bizarre, uneven mix of gray, black and white, and shot out of his head at weird, spiky angles, dark gray with white tips at the front, black and white bands everywhere else. The overall effect, especially the way his hair shot out over his eyes, pointing both outward and up, reminded Amelia of something. She just couldn't quite figure out what.

"Just don't look him in the eye, in the eye, and you'll be fine, fine, fine," the kid said, shoving his glasses up his nose, peering closely at his own computer monitor.

Amelia rubbed her arm, marveling at the strength of such a scrawny kid. She wanted to scold him for manhandling her, but the truth was, she was grateful to have escaped Mr. Fox's fury.

Determined to follow the kid's advice, Amelia slouched down in her seat and avoided looking at the teacher as he droned on and on about lines of code.

Toward the end of class, a flash of orange caught Amelia's attention and she realized a girl was sitting at the computer to her left. She hadn't even noticed when the girl sat down. Had she been there all along? The girl's hair fell in waves of orange and black stripes down her back and she sat so still, she seemed to almost be a statue. A slight movement and Amelia caught sight of the screen.

The girl was on Facebook, but it looked weird. Amelia leaned forward to get a better look.

The girl clicked the mouse and the screen minimized. She then slowly turned her head toward Amelia, much the way Mr. Fox had done.

Amelia jumped and leaned back.

The girl's eyes were orange. There were no whites showing at all, just tiny black pupils surrounded by feral, tiger eyes.

It took a minute for Amelia to get her sudden panic under control. Once her brain kicked in, though, she had a hard time not rolling her eyes. She didn't even have to ask the girl's name. She knew it. Of course, it would be Tiger. Crazy striped hair, bizarre contacts. The girl was taking her family's adopted name a little far.

The girl growled at Amelia, a low rumbling sound.

Amelia quickly turned away and stared at the monitor. Seriously? The girl had actually growled at her. Like some wild animal. What was wrong with these people?

Staring at her monitor, Amelia remembered what her dad had said to her that morning. "I know you think the people here are strange, but they love animals," he'd said. "They devote their lives to protecting entire species of animals. What could be bad about that, Amelia? Just give them a chance, all right? Just a chance."

She'd agreed because theoretically speaking, she thought it was cool that all these people wanted to save animals and preserve the environment. But realistically speaking, that didn't change the fact that they were all nuts. Still remembering her promise, and reminding herself that Felicia hadn't been so bad once she got to know her, Amelia drew in a deep breath for courage and turned back to the girl.

"My name's Amelia," she said. "What's yours?"

Just when Amelia thought the girl wasn't going to respond, she turned and stared at Amelia again, her eyes reflecting weirdly in the light. The glint of something wild shone there for a moment and Amelia had a sudden urge to flee. She clamped down on her instincts and forced herself to continue waiting.

Finally, after an interminable silence, during which the girl simply stared Amelia down, she finally growled, "Katrina," and turned away.

Amelia swallowed, then asked, even though she knew what the answer would be, "Katrina what?"

"Tiger."

Amelia nodded and turned away. She just didn't have the courage to try to continue the conversation. She'd done enough for one day. More than enough.

antlers vs. feathers

MELVIN WAS IN a pretty good mood. Sure, his antlers had made an appearance at school today – several times, in fact – but they hadn't knocked anyone unconscious or been seen by a human, so all in all, he considered the day to be not half-bad.

Now he and his best friend, Paulie, were hanging out at Paulie's house. They were supposed to be doing homework, but really Melvin was there because he needed to talk to someone about the human. Amelia.

Paulie was going on and on about some girl in his art class, but Melvin couldn't care less. He wanted to talk about Amelia. He just wasn't sure how to bring her up. He hadn't seen her once today and yet, the entire day, she was all he could think about.

How his antlers had exploded the second he caught her scent when they ran into each other at school the day before.

How they'd erupted a second time when he saw her in the library.

How they hadn't popped out at all when she caught him naked

in the woods.

How she'd given him a hard time about "skinny dipping," but then told him it was cool.

How she'd pestered him for things to do around town that were fun.

How absolutely certain he was that she would learn their secret, sending the entire town into chaos.

"She sat beside me in my tech class," Paulie announced.

"Uh-huh." It was so frustrating. His stupid antlers were going to keep him from getting to know Amelia better. He wasn't sure he liked her, but he wasn't sure he didn't like her either. It'd be nice to find out.

"I kind of had to rescue her from Mr. Fox. Honestly, the town council's delusional. There's no way that girl's not gonna figure things out."

Wait. What was Paulie going on about? "What girl?"

"The human. The girl in my art and tech classes."

Seriously? The girl Paulie had been talking about this entire time was Amelia? "Amelia's in your classes?"

"Haven't you been listening to a word I've been saying, saying? Yes, the human's in my classes and she's definitely going to figure things out."

Considering Melvin had already come to the same conclusion, he couldn't really argue the point. "Probably so. Unless she's stupid."

Paulie smirked. "I doubt she's stupid."

Melvin laughed. This was why he and Paulie were such good friends. Their thoughts often aligned. "Yeah, she's not stupid, guaranteed. Annoying, yes. Stupid, no."

"Wait. How do you know she's annoying? I thought you guys didn't even talk before … you know."

"I knocked her unconscious?"

"Well, yeah."

"We didn't."

"So you gave her a concussion —"

"I didn't give her a concussion!"

"And she's the annoying one?"

"There were no concussions and yes, she's annoying. She's a pain in my hooves!"

"In what way?"

Melvin shrugged and looked up at the ceiling, avoiding Paulie's gaze.

"No way. You met her again, didn't you? Again, again. How'd that happen? How do you keep running into this girl? I thought the counselors were supposed to make sure your schedules never cross paths, paths."

"I don't want to talk about it."

"Come on, Melvin. I'm your best friend! You're supposed to share this stuff with me."

"You'll just laugh."

Paulie grinned. "It's a funny story? Even better, even better!"

"Forget it."

"No, come on. I won't laugh. Unless she saw your antlers this time. Oh, jeez, *did* she see your antlers, antlers?"

"No, but she pretty much saw everything else."

"What does that mean? Oh my god, did she see your moose, moose?"

"Technically, yes."

"For the love of acorns, share already!"

"I don't know." Melvin hesitated. Never mind that he'd come here planning to tell Paulie the entire story. He was enjoying making him work for it.

"Come on!"

"Nope."

"I won't laugh."

Of course, he'd laugh.

"Really, I won't."

"Don't make promises you can't keep."

"Just tell me!"

"Fine." So Melvin, with much drama, began to detail the events of the evening before – leaving school as a moose, trying to retrieve his bookbag, being unable to shift back, Amelia finding him in the woods. Naked.

"Wait. Like completely naked, naked?"

"It's not like my moose was wearing shorts when I shifted, for hooves' sake!"

"And your antlers didn't make an appearance?"

"Nope. They were completely MIA."

"So what'd she say? I mean, you were naked, man!"

"She told me I was hot, of course, and then she asked if I wanted to go out."

"What? No way, no way! That's just not right."

"I told her no, of course. I mean, can you imagine what people would say if they saw me out on a date with the human? Everyone in town keeps reminding me to stay away from her. It's really annoying."

"Seriously, come on, Melvin. She didn't really ask you out, did she?"

Melvin burst out laughing. "Of course not. She turned her back and told me to get dressed."

"So it's okay if I ask her out then?"

"Wait, what? No! Come on, Paulie, you're my best friend. You don't get to date someone I can't even talk to!"

"But I like her, man."

"I don't care. I like her too, but do you see me dating her?" Wait, what was he saying? He didn't like her. He didn't even know her!

"Of course not! She'd discover the truth in about two seconds if you were dating her, dating her!"

"Hey now, I have more control than that."

Paulie just stared at him.

Melvin groaned and flung himself back onto the lower bunk. "Well, I want to have control anyway. What in all that is furry am I going to do, Paulie? I just cannot deal with these ridiculous antlers anymore. Why couldn't I have been a peacock like my mom?"

"Seriously? A peacock? You realize instead of dealing with rampaging antlers, you'd be busting feathers from your rump if you were a peacock."

Melvin lifted his head and stared at Paulie. After a second, the two burst into laughter.

"Jeez," Paulie wheezed. "Can you just see Laney Siamese's face?"

Melvin roared and rolled on the bed. "I can hear her now. Instead of 'Get those antlers out of my face, Melvin Moose'," Melvin spoke in a haughty falsetto, mimicking Laney, "it'd be, 'Get those tail feathers away from my friend's boobs, Melvin Peacock!'"

"Wait. What friend would that be?"

"Shift if I know. Whatever friend's standing behind me, getting a chestful of feathers."

seven

normal

THAT NIGHT, AS Amelia lay in bed, she made a list in her head of all the people she'd met so far, trying to figure out if it was just her imagination or if everyone really was as strange as she thought.

Katrina Tiger. Unfriendly in the extreme. Freaky contacts. Growled at her.

The kid in tech. Scrawny but strong. Warned her not to make eye contact with the teacher. Spoke in repetitive phrases.

Mr. Fox. Scary. Also growled at her. Furious that she was in his class.

Felicia and Luis. Funny. Obsessed with lettuce and bouncing. Hated salad dressing. Possibly the only two kids in school Amelia currently liked.

The P.E. teacher. Freakishly huge. Refused to allow her to take his class. Maybe because he made the students play sports without their clothes on? That just didn't sound right. But he did tell that one kid to get naked.

Amelia shook her head. She wasn't going to figure that one out anytime soon. Moving on.

Laney Siamese. Haughty. Called Amelia a freaky little human. Why did everyone keep saying that word? Final count was twenty-three – and that was just today. Not normal.

The jerk who sniffed her hair in calculus and called her prey. Disturbing.

The naked guy in the woods. What was his name – Melvin? Actually, as Amelia thought about it, she didn't really know too much about Melvin, other than his tendency to skinny dip in shallow streams.

Amelia's last thought as she drifted off to sleep was that, in the grand scheme of things, Melvin was perhaps the most normal of all the people she'd met so far.

eight

mr. sloth

AMELIA WALKED INTO her history class the next morning, exhausted and a little wary. She hadn't paid much attention in class the last few days. She'd been too busy trying to keep a low profile. Of all her classes, though, history was the one that seemed the least scary. Perhaps it was because it was first thing in the morning and most of the kids were still a bit bleary-eyed. Or maybe it was because of the teacher.

Mr. Sloth had gray hair, not really human gray, more like sloth gray. He wore glasses and kind of walked with a little hunch forward.

Like a sloth.

He also spoke really slowly. At first, Amelia had thought it was a joke – you know, Mr. Sloth acting like a real sloth. But then it just went on and on and on that first day. And then it went on and on and on yesterday as well. Now she was pretty sure it wasn't a joke.

Mr. Sloth, like everyone else in this crazy school, took his animal name just a bit too far.

While normally Amelia preferred to hang out with people who weren't sheep, following everyone else's lead, that didn't feel like the case here. These people were all not-normal in the exact same way, which meant, in some weird kind of fashion, that Amelia was the not-normal one here.

Everyone dyed their hair, wore contacts and acted in ways very similar to the animals they'd adopted. She wanted to think it was pretty cool – that these people loved animals so much, they'd go to extreme lengths to demonstrate their solidarity with the animal kingdom.

It wasn't cool though. *They* weren't cool. Instead, they were over-the-top crazy. Maybe not psychopath-crazy (though the verdict was still out on a couple of them), but still a bit nutters all the same.

She especially didn't like the way people kept throwing around the word human. It made her think she'd fallen into a *Twilight* novel. Which she absolutely refused to accept. She was not living any kind of weird supernatural anything. There was a perfectly logical explanation for everything and she was going to figure it out.

Maybe her dad was wrong. Maybe the town wasn't a wildlife sanctuary, but instead was a sanctuary for the criminally insane. Or maybe the entire town was a cult. Actually that sounded about right. A cult of animal worshippers.

Oh my god. Why hadn't she thought of this before? It made perfect sense. How to prove it though.

Also, was being in a cult that bad? Well, most cults were, but only because they brainwashed people. There were probably some cults that weren't that bad. Like nudist colonies. Those were kind of like cults. Probably people who lived in nudist colonies were thrilled to walk around naked all day. And really, it wasn't illegal, she didn't think, not if everyone there was happy to be naked. Also, people who lived off the land and had no electricity could maybe be considered a kind of cult. It was a lifestyle choice that everyone shared.

So maybe her dad was right and she should stop worrying about everything and just go with the flow. It could be kind of cool, taking part in a freaky, animal-worshipping cult. As long as they didn't slaughter animals (unlikely since they worshipped them), or require human sacrifice (in this town, the verdict was still out on that one), she was willing to give it a try.

"Hey. Amelia." Luis dropped into the desk beside her. He turned to her and grinned.

"Hi, Luis. I didn't realize you were in this class with me."

"Yeah, you were a little quiet the last two days. I was glad to meet you yesterday at lunch." As he spoke, his legs bopped up and down, his heels leaving the floor in continual small bounces. "So how are you doing? Adjusting to life in Shifferville?" He drew out the 'f' in a pronounced way, so that it sounded more like Shifffffferville.

"Um, yeah. It's an interesting place."

The bell rang before he could reply and Mr. Sloth slowly

stepped his way to the podium.

"Does he always move that slow?" Amelia whispered.

Luis studied Mr. Sloth closely. "I don't know," he murmured. "He's looking pretty spry today. Some days, it can take up to 15 minutes for him to get his lecture started."

"Please tell me you're joking."

Luis laughed.

Mr. Sloth began his lecture, keeping Amelia from finding out whether Luis was serious about Mr. Sloth's slow-moving ways.

As the minutes inched by, Mr. Sloth droning on and on about the Civil War, Amelia took notes and worried that this history class would only ever cover about ten years of history, given the methodical, slow delivery of its content.

She had to force herself to write down every word Mr. Sloth said. It was the only way she managed to stay awake.

The bell rang signaling the end of class, but no one moved. Mr. Sloth continued with his lecture as if he hadn't heard the bell.

Luis leaned over and murmured, "Don't worry. This happens all the time."

"Really? He finished on time yesterday and the day before."

"Yeah and none of us could believe it. We're pretty sure it was all your fault."

"My fault?"

"Yeah, he was on his best behavior trying to impress the –"

"The what?"

"The new girl."

"Well, this new girl's going to be late for class."

"Yeah, no worries. Just tell your teacher Mr. Sloth wasn't finished with his lecture. They all know how he is."

Amelia didn't like that plan at all. She had art with Mrs. Spider next.

Mr. Sloth finally stopped talking and very slowly closed the history book he'd been lecturing from. He slowly tilted his head up, smiled at the class, and said, "Well, that's all today, class." He spoke slowly and carefully, enunciating each word. "Have a nice day."

The students all stood at once and bolted for the classroom door. The bell rang as the first student hit the hallway.

Amelia followed everyone out, unwilling to try to shove her way through the mass of students.

She had just reached the door when another student pushed his way inside.

It was Melvin.

In clothes this time.

escape

MELVIN SCENTED HER first. He tried to step back, but there were students everywhere, all shoving forward, trying to make it inside the classroom, and then it was too late.

He stood face to face with Amelia.

This just wasn't possible. He couldn't believe the counselors had done this to him.

Amelia's eyes lit up when she saw him. "Hi, Melvin!"

Dungit.

Melvin clapped his hands to his head, swung around and shoved his way through the mass of bodies.

His classmates parted for him swiftly.

Probably didn't want to become his latest antler victim.

As soon as the path opened, Melvin took off at a dead run. He made it around the corner just as his antlers exploded.

The right one slammed into the row of lockers, knocking him to the left. Thankfully, the bell had already rung, so there weren't any students to flatten as he fell sideways.

He flung out an arm, shoved off the lockers to his left and staggered forward.

"Melvin?"

Fantlers, she was following him.

Melvin poured on the speed and hurtled down the hallway. He slid around the corner, saw an open door, and, not even caring which classroom it was, he barreled inside.

Paulie was the first person he saw. Then he noticed the easels and canvases. Scat! This wasn't art class, was it?

"Melvin Moose, what are you doing?" Mrs. Spider glowered at him from her spot at the front of the room.

"Mrs. Spider, I'm–my antlers–the human–she–" Melvin leaned forward to put his hands on his knees and his antlers knocked over an easel. He jerked upright and a painting came with him. He reached up, but couldn't quite reach the painting. "Sorry–sorry–she's out there–she's going to see–I need to–" he swung in a circle. There was nowhere to hide. Nowhere. Where was he going to hide?

Paulie stood. "Where is she?"

Melvin pointed to the door, still trying to figure out where he could go. The windows! He hurried toward them. They should be wide enough, though he might have to–BAM!

Melvin grabbed his head and staggered back. Dammit. He'd rammed his brow tines into the glass.

Paulie walked to the door, peeked out, then stepped back in. "She's out there, all right. I think Katrina's distracting her."

Melvin blanched. That probably wasn't a good thing. Katrina could be a bit abrasive. Still, if Katrina had delayed Amelia, he owed her big. "She saw me. Not my antlers, but she was leaving history just as I was going in and–"

"Melvin Moose!"

"Yes, Mrs. Spider?"

"I'm going out there to deal with the human. You figure things out. Get those antlers under control right now, young man!"

Melvin nodded and almost tipped over again. Staggering forward, he flung his head back, overcompensating by about ten million, and his antlers hit the windows again. His feet slipped and he landed on the floor with a loud thud.

Mrs. Spider shook her head and pointed her finger at him. "Figure it out, Melvin. Now!"

The minute the door closed behind Mrs. Spider, Paulie bolted to Melvin's side. "Jake, help me!"

Jake leapt forward and with the ease of experience, the two of them ducked under Melvin's antlers, grabbed an arm each and hauled him upright.

"What's the plan?" Jake asked.

"Window."

Paulie looked at the window, then back at Melvin. "Not sure you're gonna fit, man."

"Just open the dewlapped window."

Shaking his head, Paulie unlatched the window and shoved it outward. "You're never going to fit, Melvin. Maybe if the entire pane wasn't here, but it only opens so far, safety you know."

"Guys, you'd better hurry!" Kayla called from the door. "Mrs. Spider's on her way back and the human's with her!"

Melvin cursed, shoved Paulie out of the way, tipped his head back, grabbed the window pane and shoved with all his moose strength. There was a loud crack and the hinge holding the window in place, keeping it from opening too far, broke loose. Another shove and the entire window broke away and fell.

Not hesitating, Melvin climbed up onto the window sill, turned sideways, tilted his head one way, then the other and finally managed to get one antler through the window. He tried to do the same for the other, but that stupid painting was still hanging on his antler. "Paulie!"

"Yeah, yeah, got it." Paulie climbed onto a shelf, grabbed the painting and with a jerk detached it from Melvin's rack, sending it to the floor with a clatter.

Melvin twisted, turned, and pulled until with a loud clang, his rack sprang free, unbalancing Melvin and sending him off the ledge with a yelp.

Melvin landed on his back with enough force, all the breath was expelled from his lungs. His rack hit the ground beneath him, rattling his brain for about the seventeen millionth time that morning.

Paulie leaned out the window above him. "You okay, Melvin?"

Melvin gave him a thumbs up, still trying to catch his breath. Thank goodness art was on the first floor because he wasn't sure he would have survived anything higher.

"Paulie Porcupine! Get down from there this instant!"

Paulie grinned at Melvin and disappeared back into the classroom.

Melvin slowly rolled over and belly crawled his way beneath the windows, crawling and crawling until he was certain he was far enough away from the art classroom, he wouldn't be visible to anyone looking out its windows. He slowly sat up and set his back against the wall. He leaned forward and settled his head into his hands. He needed to focus. Just focus.

The minutes ticked by slowly as he tried to convince his moose that antlers were not a requirement at the moment.

His moose, however, was a stubborn pain in the rump.

stalking melvin

AMELIA COULDN'T BELIEVE it when Melvin just bolted. He looked horrified and then he turned and ran.

Surely it wasn't because of her. Maybe he'd forgotten his homework or something. Or maybe he got sick all of a sudden.

Pushing her way through the mob of students trying to enter the classroom, Amelia caught a glimpse of Melvin just before he disappeared around a corner.

She raced after him, calling his name, but only caught a glimpse of something sliding around the next corner before a girl stepped into her path.

Amelia slid to a stop.

It was Katrina Tiger.

Amelia smiled, "Hi, Katrina."

Katrina just glowered at her, orange eyes pretty much freaking Amelia out.

"Did you want something?"

No answer.

"Okay, well. It's great to see you, Katrina, but I need to get to my next class." Amelia slid around Katrina and turned the corner. She stopped and looked around. No Melvin.

"What class?" Katrina's low and raspy voice came from behind her.

Amelia turned around, surprised that Katrina had deigned to follow, let alone speak with her.

"Um. Art."

Katrina shook her head.

"No?"

"Not yet."

"I can't go to art yet?"

"No."

"Why not?"

Katrina didn't answer.

"Katrina?"

No answer.

"Well, if that's all, I really should get to class." Amelia took a step back.

"We should hang out."

Amelia wasn't sure which of them was more surprised by this statement. Katrina looked about as stunned as Amelia felt. "Um, sure, Katrina, that'd be great. I need to go to class now, but maybe after school—"

"Now."

"I'm sorry. What?"

"Now. We should skip class, hang out now."

Amelia didn't know how to respond to this. It was so outside the realm of anything she might have expected from Katrina. It was probably a setup. That was the only explanation. A scene straight from a retro *Carrie* movie was surely next. "I'm not really one to skip school."

"Why not?"

Amelia had to think about that.

There were so many reasons not to skip school and about a million more for why she shouldn't do it with Katrina. Which reason to give that wouldn't offend though. "I just don't like to fall behind in my classes."

"Oh, come on. We'll have fun." Katrina stepped forward and did just about the scariest thing Amelia could have possibly imagined. She slung her arm around Amelia's shoulders like they were the best of friends.

"Katrina Tiger! What are you doing out here? You should be in class."

Thank goodness. That was Mrs. Spider, the art teacher.

"And you, young lady, what is your name again, oh, yes, Amelia. What are you doing out here?"

"Well, um, Mr. Sloth dismissed class a little late, but then I, um–" Amelia didn't want to get Katrina in trouble, so she said the only thing she could think of. "I got a little turned around, went down the wrong hall, and Katrina here was kind enough to show me the way."

Mrs. Spider just stared at her. She was a very tall, very thin woman. Her legs and arms were super long and her face was narrow. Her hair was pitch black, with random white strands throughout.

Finally, Mrs. Spider looked at Katrina. "Is that true, Katrina?"

"Yes, ma'am."

"Very well. Get to class, young lady."

"Yes, ma'am."

"Now, Amelia, I wanted a moment to speak with you anyway."

"You did?"

"Yes, dear. Which medium do you like to work in the most? Where do you feel your artistic talents lie?"

"Oh, um, I'm not sure." Amelia had never had an art teacher ask her this before. "I mostly enjoy drawing, with almost any utensil – pencils, colored or not, pens, charcoal, graphite. I also like to play around in digital drawing programs."

Mrs. Spider nodded. "That all sounds lovely. Any experience with sculpture or painting?"

"Just in the occasional art unit."

"Jewelry making? Glass blowing?"

"No, but that'd be cool."

"All right. The way art works here at Shiffer High, is you pretty much direct your own studies. I will provide the materials you need, the models you need, but you determine your medium, your supplies, your representation of art."

"Wow. That's really cool."

"Yes, it is. Let's get to class now." She led the way to her door, talking as she went. "So, my dear, think about what you would like to study in art this year, what materials you might need, and we'll speak again."

"Okay. Thank you."

"And, dear," Mrs. Spider stopped at her classroom door. "Do try to be on time from now on."

"Yes, ma'am."

"I understand about Mr. Sloth, so do yourself a favor and learn the path between these two classrooms, make sure you have everything you will need for art, and when he dismisses class, come straight here, no delays."

"Yes, ma'am."

With a brisk nod, Mrs. Spider opened the classroom and immediately began shouting, "Paulie Porcupine! Get down from there this instant!"

the scarf

"NO, MELVIN."

Why wouldn't she listen? "Mrs. Husky, you have to help me. Everyone's telling me to stay away from the human, but I can't do that if I'm running into her every morning between first and second hour. You know how Mr. Sloth is – he'll be letting them out late all the time!"

"Melvin, we've already changed her schedule once. We just can't do it again without raising her suspicions. If you want to change your schedule, that I can do."

"I don't want to change my schedule! Every option you've shown me means I have to drop choir!"

"Then you're just going to have to control your antlers better, young man. There's no excuse for the constant displays. Gain control of your shift, Melvin."

As if it were that easy. No one understood. "How am I supposed to do that?"

"Well how would I know? I'm not a moose! Maybe it's time to

ask your father for some advice."

What a perfectly dreadful idea. It was just the sort of conversation Melvin had been avoiding.

"Well?"

"I'll figure things out," Melvin muttered, turning away. He couldn't believe that was her solution. Like talking to his father would solve anything. His dad was a great guy, but basically a giant nerd. Melvin was pretty sure if his dad had ever had any issue with his antlers, he probably hadn't been bothered by them or really even noticed the issue at all.

He'd just have to come up with some other plan.

Leaving the counseling office, Melvin trudged down the hallway, completely dejected. Mrs. Husky hadn't even given him a pass to class. Mr. Sloth might be cool, but even he'd raise an eyebrow at Melvin's tardiness today.

As he turned the corner, he noticed a slash of red on the floor outside the history door.

Leaning over, Melvin picked up the scarf and straightening, reached for the doorknob.

The amazing scent of Amelia barreled over him and he swung away from the classroom door, clapping both hands to his head.

Which meant the scarf brushed against his nose and he inhaled a stronger dose of human.

Clang!

His antlers barreled free, slamming into the row of lockers, once again ringing his bell.

And he was done.

Melvin huffed out a breath, swung around and plopped down on the ground. He leaned back against the lockers and ran Amelia's scarf through his hands.

If she came around the corner, he wasn't even going to run.

Let her see him in all his moosetastic glory!

He didn't even care anymore.

twelve

the problem with peacocks

MELVIN WAS STILL depressed at dinner that night. Why was it all on him to make sure the human didn't discover their secrets? Why couldn't the town council have just said no? It was stupid to invite a couple humans to live here.

"What's the matter, darling? Aren't you enjoying the shrub stew?"

Melvin shrugged. "It's fine, Mom." To prove it, he scooped up a spoonful and swallowed it down. Truthfully, it was delicious. His mother was an amazing cook. She did something with the bark and the shrubs, some sort of seasoning that gave it a bit of spice. He was just too busy worrying about running into Amelia outside Mr. Sloth's room every day for the rest of the year to enjoy his dinner. It would serve the town right if he just let his antlers out, let her see the truth. She was going to find out eventually. Might as well be because of him.

"Are you sure, sweetheart? Everything okay at school?"

"Yeah, everything's fine." If busting his antlers out every other class and having to run from the human anytime he saw her counted as fine. Everyone would blame him if she found out because of his antlers.

"How's the antler situation, son?"

Oh, great. Now his father had joined the conversation and he wanted to talk about Melvin's antlers. Embarrassing enough to discuss the situation with his dad, but at the dinner table? In front of his mom? Melvin shrugged and didn't look up from his bowl.

"I heard you requested a schedule change."

Jeez, was nothing sacred in this town? Everyone knew everyone else's business. It was so annoying. Even worse because Melvin's dad had worked at the high school for years as a math teacher. When Melvin advanced to the high school, his dad had requested a transfer to the middle school, something for which Melvin would be eternally grateful. His dad really was cool that way. Still, because he'd worked at the high school for so many years, he had a ton of contacts who kept him apprised of Melvin's every move.

"Melvin, why did you ask for a schedule change?" his mom asked.

"It wasn't for me. It was for the human, Amelia."

"I don't understand."

Melvin huffed in exasperation. "She's in Mr. Sloth's first hour class. I'm in his second hour."

"You're kidding me." His dad shook his head in disbelief.

"I know, right? And Mrs. Husky wouldn't change her schedule.

She said I'd have to change mine, but the only option meant giving up choir. I'm not giving up choir, Dad!"

"Of course not!" Melvin's mom was completely into the arts. She'd signed Melvin up for music lessons when he was just three years old. He'd been singing and playing the piano ever since. Truthfully, Melvin enjoyed the music and he was good at it, which meant it was an easy A. He wasn't giving it up just because some human moved to town.

"Dad, you've gotta help me!" Oh Jeez. Now he'd done it. What had happened to his determination to never ask his dad for advice on this situation? Clearly he'd lost his mind.

"Help you with what, Melvin?" His dad's eyes lit up. That was the thing about Melvin's dad. He loved problem-solving. He treated everything like a mathematical equation, every situation just a problem to be unraveled and solved. Like Melvin's antler situation would ever be so easily figured out. "What's the problem?"

Melvin sighed. Might as well get it over with. "I hate my antlers!" Not exactly what he'd meant to say, but true nonetheless.

"Now, Melvin. They're not that bad, darling."

"They're a nightmare, Mom, a total nightmare. You should have married another peacock!"

"A peacock! Oh, Melvin, I would never. Your father was the most handsome bull at school. Once I met him, none of the other boys stood a chance, especially not the peacocks with all their strutting around and preening. Not a single thought in their heads but attracting the hens. Your father, though, he was so incredibly intelligent." She smiled at his dad. "I was attracted to his brain as much as to his sexy body."

"Oh, Mom, gross." Ugh. The look on her face as she stared at his dad was revolting. Great. Now he'd have to see if he could stay at Paulie's tonight. No way did he want to be in the house now.

Ever since he'd gotten old enough to understand what it meant when his parents were "wrestling," their two thousand square foot home just wasn't big enough for the three of them. His dad's mating bellow was just freaking disturbing. Great. Now his thoughts were going to really unhealthy places.

"So, how am I supposed to help you again?" Bless his father for his one-track mind.

"Just tell me how you dealt with your antlers, Dad. How did you finally gain control of them?"

"Gain control? Melvin, what are you talking about?"

"My antlers showing up when they're not needed! Just tell me what you did to stop the partial shifts."

"Partial– Melvin, I don't know how to break it to you, but I never had the issues you're having."

"What?"

"Yeah, I've never heard of a moose experiencing partial shifts like this. It's just something unique to you, I guess."

"Unique to – well, what makes me so dung special?"

"Melvin! Watch your language!"

"Sorry, Mom, but come on! Why am I the one struggling with antlers popping out all over the place? Why not Dad? Why not his moose friends from high school? Why just me?"

"Why, Melvin, haven't you figured it out yet?" His mom looked surprised.

"Figured what out?"

"It's because you're a peacock, darling."

"I'm not a peacock. I'm a moose."

"Yes, yes, your shifted form is that of a moose, but surely you didn't think you received no peacock traits. It doesn't work that way, sweetheart. You're as much my son as you are your father's."

"What does that have to do with anything?"

"It's the peacock in you."

"What's the peacock in me?"

"When I was your age, all the peacocks would strut around the school, in their shifted forms, feathers flying high. It was their way of enticing the girls, you see. Not that I had eyes for them at all. All I could see was your great bull of a father."

"Oh, gah, Mom, please, not with that again."

"He was so handsome."

"Mom, back to my problem, please. I don't understand what my antlers have to do with peacocks."

"It's their way, Melvin. Your mother's trying to tell you that it's the peacock in you forcing the partial shift."

"I didn't even know I had a peacock in me. And even if you're right, why would the peacock force my antlers out?"

"Because you have no tail feathers to show off, dear. So your peacock has elected your antlers to serve in their place."

"Wait a minute. Are you telling me that all these partial shifts are because of the peacock in me, not because I'm out of control?"

"You're in perfect control, Melvin. Your peacock wants your antlers out to impress the girls."

"But I don't want them out! They're not impressing anyone, Mom. Isn't there a way to make it stop happening?"

"I really don't think so. It's just who you are, sweetheart. You have to accept that you're not just a moose. You're also a peacock. With those two animals come many varied, wonderful traits."

"Wonderful, my rump!"

"Melvin!"

"Sorry," he muttered, "but this sucks." Silence fell as Melvin pondered what all this meant. He was completely dewlapped and Paulie was right. *I really would have had feathers sprouting from my rump.*

"So—"

"Yeah." Melvin stared at the ceiling and tried to ignore Paulie's snickers from above. The bunks they sprawled across were in an L-shape, so Paulie's top bunk was against one wall while Melvin's lower bunk was against another. Any minute now, Paulie would swing his head over the rail to continue the conversation. It wouldn't happen until he was done laughing though.

"So your antlers are going to be impressing girls your entire life, life?" Paulie's words were garbled, he was laughing so hard. Still Melvin understood exactly what he'd said.

"Unfortunately, yes." He suddenly had a vision of himself as a crotchety old moose-man, 93 years old, stooped over and walking with a cane. He'd be on the sidewalk of their town and a young woman would brush by and BAM!

Antler hell.

At 93.

Shameful.

His entire life was going to be a series of humiliating events and there was nothing he could do about it.

"So what's the plan, Melvin?" Paulie swung his head over the side of the bunk and stared at him, just as Melvin had predicted. "You're going to see Amelia in the morning."

"Only if Mr. Sloth releases class late."

Paulie just stared at him.

Melvin huffed. "Yeah. I know. It's a miracle when he doesn't keep us past the bell."

"So what's your plan?"

"I don't have one. I don't know what I'm gonna do. Maybe I should just go to Sloth's class late every day."

"Not a good idea."

"I know, but what else can I do?"

"Well, what did you do to keep your antlers from showing up when Amelia found you in the woods?"

"Nothing. Not really. I mean, I'd already shifted a lot of times that day and I just got stuck. I couldn't shift back."

"That's it, man!" Paulie jumped down from the top bunk. "That's your solution, solution!"

"What are you talking about?" Melvin sat up.

"Shift over and over again before school until you can't shift anymore. That would work, right, right, right?"

"I-I don't know. Maybe."

"Well, we should try tomorrow. It'll be an experiment."

Melvin nodded. "Yeah, yeah, that's a great idea." If it worked, then he could actually have a civil conversation with Amelia, maybe even get to know her.

"How many times do you think it'll take?"

"I'm not sure. I guess I'll just play it by ear."

Paulie climbed back up to the top bunk. "We'll get up early, shift a bunch of times. This is going to be great, great, man!"

Melvin wasn't sure great was the right word. He didn't really like the idea of not being able to shift when he wanted to. It felt like he'd be crippling his moose. On the other hand, attending classes even one day without worrying about the unexpected appearances of his rampant rack sounded absolutely wonderful.

the study

MELVIN SHOULD HAVE just gone home when he woke that morning.

Instead, he'd joined Paulie and his family for breakfast. Now there wasn't enough time for Melvin to go home and shift a bunch of times before getting to school. If he wanted to conduct their experiment, he was going to have to do it at Paulie's house.

This was a problem.

Unlike Melvin's house, which was quite large to accommodate the occasional moose shift, Paulie's house was much smaller. The only room large enough to accommodated a shifted Melvin was the study, which belonged to Paulie's dad.

Paulie suggested the backyard, but Melvin refused to conduct their experiment where Paulie's neighbors might see them.

Which was how Melvin ended up inside Mr. Porcupine's study, undressing.

Luckily, Mr. Porcupine had already left for work and Paulie's mom was busy getting his younger brothers and sisters ready for school. This allowed Melvin and Paulie the freedom to sneak into Mr. Porcupine's study without being seen.

Melvin had never been in the study before. It was a large room with a reading nook on one side and Mr. Porcupine's desk on the other. Between the two areas was a large empty, carpeted space.

"The kids like to play on the carpet," Paulie explained. "Do you think it's a big enough space for your moose?"

"Probably." Melvin eyed the area. "Maybe we should move the armchairs a little further back. The desk too. Just in case." He really didn't want to destroy Mr. Porcupine's study with his ridiculously large moose form.

"Right, let's do it then."

Once they'd moved the furniture, Melvin felt better. "I think this should be enough room," he said, "especially if I don't move around a lot."

"Right, okay. Well, I'm going to stand in the hall, keep a lookout. You shift as many times as you can, as quickly as possible. You've got about fifteen minutes before we have to leave."

"Got it." Melvin was already pulling off his clothes. He barely registered when Paulie left, closing the door behind him.

As soon as he was naked, Melvin focused on his moose form. As usual, the first shift of the day was the fastest and the easiest. Melvin's moose exploded from his human form, antlers slamming into the walls on either side.

Melvin froze. Was his rack seriously so long that it stretched from wall to wall?

He slowly turned his head, the clatter of his points as they scraped across the walls making him cringe.

He froze again. Did it really matter how long his spread was? What mattered was shifting back.

He focused on his human form and the sound of his bones breaking and shrinking filled the room, along with the sound of several things falling to the floor.

Please don't let that be anything important.

His knees buckled and he landed on the carpet, gasping for breath.

He looked up and winced. His antlers had scraped some paint from one of the walls and– he glanced to the other wall–oops.

A knock sounded on the door. "Everything okay in there, Melvin?" Paulie stuck his head in.

"Um, yeah, just knocked over a shelf of books."

"No worries. You done shifting yet?"

"I don't think so."

"Okay, well, hurry it up. You're down to ten minutes." Paulie closed the door again, leaving Melvin alone in the study.

He debated choosing a new position. Was it better to stay where he'd been to minimize damage elsewhere or find a new place where his antlers wouldn't cause issues?

Melvin pushed to his feet. He wasn't sure there was anywhere else he could stand. The study that had seemed so large before now seemed really small. He should have gone home last night, never mind his parents' plans for the evening.

Planting his feet, Melvin focused on his moose. It was harder this time. Not hard enough though. He shifted and shifted back. Then he did it again. Three full shifts should do it, right?

He thought about Amelia – the smile on her face when she'd seen him yesterday, the skeptical look she'd given him in the woods, the way she'd smelled. His head got that tingling that signaled an impending partial shift.

"Dammit," Melvin muttered. "One more time."

He focused on his moose form. The antlers came first this time in his hated partial shift. He swayed in place, the points rattling against the bookshelf on one side and the wall on the other as he tried not to let the weight of his rack drag him to the floor.

Bullwinkle.

Where was his moose?

Just as he had that thought, the rest of the form followed, legs cracking and bending and reforming, then his chest, arms, and last his head. It was the slowest and most painful shift he'd ever experienced.

When it was over, his back legs went out from under him and he landed on his rump.

As he went down, one antler collapsed two more shelves and the points of his other antler dragged a furrow in the wall, expanding the damage already there.

"Melvin, we're out of time." Paulie opened the door. "We've gotta go, go, go. Come on, big guy. Time to be human again."

Melvin tried to remember what it was like to shift back to

human, tried to picture his human form, tried to force that shift, but his human form had never seemed so far away.

"Melvin, this really isn't cool, isn't cool, man." Paulie slid into the room, closed the door and leaned against it to study Melvin. "You're stuck, stuck, stuck, aren't you?"

Melvin lifted his chin, just a little, dewlap swaying a bit with the movement. He was reluctant to move much beyond that, out of fear that he'd cause even more damage to Mr. Porcupine's study.

Paulie sighed. "Guess we're gonna be late, be late." He slid down the door and settled on the floor.

Melvin blinked. He couldn't believe Paulie was going to keep him company, rather than go to school. Paulie hated to be late for anything, let alone for a class. He considered it rude. Yet Paulie was staying rather than rushing off.

Of course, Melvin was stuck in his moose form in Paulie's dad's study. Paulie was probably worried Melvin would destroy the entire room if left alone.

"So. Think about your human form. Your monstrously huge feet. Your gangly arms and freakishly long legs. Your ugly head – you know the one. The antler-free, *human* one. Focus on those and shift, shift."

Melvin just stared at him.

"Yeah, yeah, I know you know this, but you gotta focus, Melvin. Focus, focus, focus!"

Melvin didn't want to focus. He wanted to lie down. The only thing he wanted to focus on was a nap. Just for a little while. A small, tiny nap.

"No, no, no, no, no, no, no!"

Melvin jerked and his antlers made a screeching sound as they scraped along the study's wall and bookshelf.

"You can't go to sleep, Melvin. We have to get to school, school. Besides, if you nap in here, you'll take out the rest of my dad's bookshelves and probably his desk too on your way down, on your way down."

That was true. Melvin was so tired, but no nap. No nap meant he had to sit here, in his moose form, with his heavy antlers to hold up, unable to even lean over or relax.

"Melvin, Melvin!"

Melvin jerked again. Right. He needed to shift. Because staying here, in his moose form, awake, was never gonna happen. He needed to shift or he needed a nap. Frankly, he needed both.

He pictured his hand reaching out and grabbing his moose form, hauling those antlers back inside, shoving his moose deep, pulling out the human form.

His moose form slowly shrank, his bones cracking and reforming. His antlers were the last to go, shrinking back into his head, scraping paint and wood as they pulled from the wall and shelf where'd they'd lodged.

Melvin fell forward, sprawling facedown across the carpet, his human form so drained of energy, he wasn't sure he'd ever manage to gain his feet again. Time whirled away in slow, steady beats.

"Come on, Melvin." Paulie dragged him to his feet. "There's

no way you're going to have gone through this for nothing. Second hour starts in thirty minutes. If we hurry, we can just make it."

Melvin glanced around. The bookshelf he'd destroyed was intact again.

"They weren't ruined, just collapsed. The wood had a few gouges, but the books mostly cover the rough spots. My dad will never notice. The wall, on the other hand we may have to repair."

They would definitely have to fix it. There were huge furrows in the wall, gouges that stretched from just below the ceiling – Melvin knew that'd be just over the seven-foot mark – to about the mid-point of the wall. "I'm so sorry, Paulie. Tell your dad it's my fault."

"It's all good. As long as we fix what we broke, my dad'll be fine. Let's get to class, and next time, maybe we'll run the experiment at your house."

"Yeah, good plan."

fourteen

the conversation

MR. SLOTH FINALLY dismissed class and Amelia bolted for the door.

She was determined to catch that Melvin kid before he ran away again.

She slid out of the classroom, ducked to the side and watched as the rest of her class shuffled out, then the next class moved in. No Melvin.

Damn.

Was he avoiding her?

Great. Now she was sounding paranoid as well as crazy. This place was getting to her.

She shook her head and pushed off the wall. Time for art.

"Amelia! Hey, Amelia!"

She swung around and watched, amazed, as Melvin staggered to a stop in front of her.

Jeez. He didn't look good. At all.

"Are you all right?"

He swayed and braced a hand against the lockers. "Yeah, I'm fine. Um, just, yeah."

Amelia waited, but he didn't say anything else. Just smiled at her, a goofy look on his face. "So did you need something?"

"Um, no. I don't think so. Why?"

"You called my name," she reminded him.

"Oh, right. So. Yeah. Jeez." And he fell silent again.

"Are you sure you're okay?"

"Apology!" he burst out.

"What?" Amelia leaned back a little, surprised at his enthusiasm.

"I wanted to – um, apologize – you know, for running like that yesterday. I realized I forgot – forgot," he fell silent again.

Wow, he really wasn't much of a conversationalist. "It's okay. I'm glad you stopped me. It's nice to see you." She grinned. "In school. With clothes on."

Red rushed up his neck, bloomed in his cheeks. God, he was cute. In a nerdy, overgrown kind of way.

The bell rang.

"Yeah, so I should probably get to class," Amelia said gently.

"Yeah." Melvin nodded. "Class."

"Okay, well, I'll see you later."

"Yeah, later."

Smiling, Amelia walked away. As she reached the end of the hall, she glanced back, saw that he was still standing there, watching her. She waved, then bolted around the corner, late for art. Again.

Melvin watched as Amelia disappeared around the corner.

For the love of dewlaps, what was wrong with him? He finally got a chance to speak with her while not battling nakedness or sudden antlerhood, and he had nothing to say. Nothing at all.

"How'd it go, big guy?"

Melvin started. "Oh, hey, Paulie. Not so great. I forgot to think about what I wanted to say."

"You didn't – what were you thinking about the entire time we were walking here then?"

"Making my feet move."

Paulie laughed. "All right, yeah. I didn't realize the shifts would take so much out of you."

"Me neither." Just thinking about going through that again tomorrow made Melvin want to puke. He wasn't sure he'd have the strength of will.

"Your antlers didn't come out though, right?"

"Right. Not even a tingle." Which now that Melvin thought about it was a dewlapping miracle.

"So the experiment worked."

"Yeah. Except I feel like scat." A complete understatement.

"But, Melvin, it worked. You had a conversation with a girl and your antlers didn't flatten her, so that's a win, right?"

Melvin thought about it a minute, then grinned. Paulie was right. For the first time since his antlers had come in, he wasn't worried about them exploding in the middle of class. For once, he could relax.

With a huge grin on his face, Melvin strode into Mr. Sloth's class while Paulie headed off for art.

Nothing could bring down his mood, not even when Mr. Sloth gave him the evil eye for his tardiness, not even when Laney Siamese sniffed her nose at him and gave him the cold shoulder in English class.

He'd conquered his antlers and he rode that high through class after class until he arrived at P.E. and Mr. Grizzly shouted, "All right, you mangy mammals! On the field, dressed out in fur, in five!"

Aw, son of a shifter!

Continue reading the Shifter High series at

www.ajculey.com/shifter-high-anthologies

special thanks to

♦ Jeanine Henning for creating the most amazing book covers and for bringing Shifter High's cast to remarkable, colorful life. Each individual book and the series as a whole would not be what they are today without her incredible talent and dedication.

♦ J.L. Troughton for being the amazing, conscientious editor that she is. While her editing skills are superb, I appreciate just as much her willingness to discuss plot points and potential storylines at any hour of the day or night. I couldn't do this work without her!

♦ Two bloggers and fellow authors, Cara McKinnon and Jennifer Loring, who hosted some of my writing on their blogs back in June of 2016. That writing later became the inspiration for the prequel novella in this book, *The Trouble with Shifter Towns*.

  • *Human-Proofing Shifter High* was originally published at caramckinnon.com/2016/06/21/guest-blog-by-a-j-culey

  • *The Rack of Destruction* was originally published at jennifertloring.com/2016/06/22/the-trouble-with-antlers-by-a-j-culey

ANTLER TROUBLE
A Shifter High Anthology

Thank you for reading Antler Trouble.

Please consider leaving a review on your favorite book site.

*

To be notified of upcoming new releases,

please sign up for A.J.'s newsletter at

www.ajculey.com/contact

Shifter High

enjoy this excerpt from the next anthology of

Shifter High

"Those rabbits will have me starving, Melvin, if they get even half a chance!"

"Please, you're not in danger of starving, Paulie."

"Why does everyone always say that? I'm not in danger only because I bury my winter stores."

"Your false winter stores."

"Sure, but I bury both. I mean, you know, I bury the real thing all quiet, where no one can find them, and I bury my false stores, still quiet, but maybe just a little not-quiet, to fool the bunnies, you see."

"What are you going on about now?"

"The bunnies, man! Those thieving, blasted bunnies. They're always stealing my winter stores."

"Well, you're burying them outside, Paulie. It's bound to happen. You're a shifter, you live in a house. Put 'em in your pantry, for heaven's sake."

"Why would I do that? Everyone knows that's where food is stored. Anyone could find it there! I keep telling my parents that, but do they listen to me? No! And my mom's a squirrel. I mean, really, 100% squirrel, and she just doesn't get it. Why doesn't anyone understand what I'm saying? Those bunnies can burrow anywhere. They can get into our house, find our winter stores in the pantry where everyone stores them, and then where will we be? In Starvation City, that's where! In the County of Cannibalism! I don't want to become a cannibal, Melvin! You should hide your food too. Everyone should hide their food!"

"Okay, calm down, Mr. Nutters. Everything's going to be just fine."

Paulie huffed. "Why does everyone keep calling me that, as if it's a bad thing? I'm a squirrel! Of course, I'm a little nutters."

"Porcupine. Let's be clear. You're a porcupine."

"*Squirrel*-porcupine!"

"Right."

BUNNYTROUBLE

is now available featuring

THE TROUBLE WITH THIEVES (a.k.a. Those Blasted Bunnies) THE TROUBLE WITH TIGERS (a.k.a. Katrina's Homicidal Urges)

other books by A.J. Culey

FOR YOUNG READERS:

Picture Books:
A Fairy's Job

If My Cat Could Fly

Salsa Visits the Zoo

Taco Runs Away

Tyrabbisaurus Rex Chapter Books:
Tyrabbisaurus Rex

Revenge of the Tiger

Zombie Bunnies

FOR YOUNG ADULT AND ADULT READERS:

Beneath the Willow:
Sehmah's Truth

Jennara in Flux

Shifter High Anthologies:
Antler Trouble

Bunny Trouble

Prickly Trouble

about the author

A.J. Culey is a teacher, world traveler and writer. She lives with a number of very bossy cats and can be found at her website www.ajculey.com She can also be followed on Facebook at www.facebook.com/ajculey.author and on Instagram and Twitter @ajculey.

T-Rab from *Tyrabbisaurus Rex* is also on Twitter and when he manages to coax the laptop away from A.J., can be found @Tyrabbisaurus.

about the illustrator

Professional cover designer and illustrator to authors and publishers worldwide, Jeanine's extensive 17 year professional background includes children's book illustration and publication, comic book art and publishing, book cover art, console game design and product branding.

She is however wondering where T-Rab took her pencils. And if in fact they still exist (she doubts it).